Genocide on Se'Yan't

A Screenplay by
Farley L. Dunn

THREE SKILLET

GENOCIDE ON SE'YAN'T, Dunn, Farley L
First Edition

A SCREENPLAY

Based on:
ALL FALL DOWN, Book 1 in
THE SE'YAN'T CHRONICLES

 THREE SKILLET
www.ThreeSkilletPublishing.com

ISBN: 978-1-943189-78-6

Genocide on Se'Yan't

Based on the Novel:

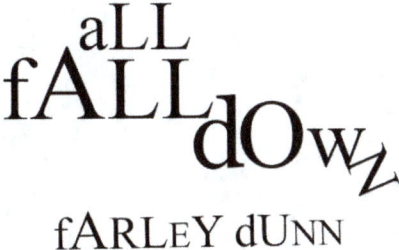

aLL
fALL dOwn

fARLEY dUNN

Table of Contents

Overview of Se'yan't

MegaCorp is the largest commercial and
military enterprise in the galaxy.

What MegaCorp wants, MegaCorp gets.

Suspicions surface that Se'Yan't has
uncovered the secret of immortality, and
MegaCorp is determined to wrest it from
the native inhabitants.

The innate cruelty of the two senior
officers of the MegaCorp ship sent to
subdue Se'Yan't's inhabitants into
submission erupts into a killing frenzy,
decimating the population to the last man,
woman, and child.

Greed is the cause. Genocide is the
result.

Except.

The natives of Se'Yan't have perhaps,
truly, kept the secret of immortality for
themselves, despite MegaCorp's plans . . .

Cast of Characters

Speaking Parts
In Order of Appearance

Rjorck, an old man
Adhor'k, Rjorck's sister
Ma'jene Holcum, UnderGen'l
Willane Bofsky, CaptGen'l
First Officer
Ma'jene Holcum, age 14-17
Rom'n Rezalton, age 14
Squad Commander
Rjorck, age 18-20
Three Elders on Se'Yan't
Crew, in transit
Banker on Earth
Le'rane, undercadet
2nd Undercadet in Shower
3rd Undercadet in Shower
Ma'jene Holcum, age 8
1st Soldier
2nd Soldier
E'vonn, Rjorck's friend
Willane Bofsky, age 12
Counselor at Academy
1st 14/15, beat up Bofsky
2nd 14/15, (Gr'gan Rh'nst)
3rd 14/15, beat up Bofsky
4th 14/15, beat up Bofsky
Teacher in science lab
Rom'n Rezalton as an Adult
Willy (Willane) Bofsky, age 10
Big Man, stepfather
Bofsky's Mother
Voice, awards ceremony
Willane Bofsky, age 17
Renhant, age 17
Jer'son, age 17

Renhant, age 17
Port Duty Officer
Rovek, duty asst. officer
Zen'ri, boy killed
Very Old Rjorck, near death
Shn'dri, Rjorck's nurse
Berian, Rjorck's friend
Rom'n Rezalton, age 13
Jo'n, Rom'n's brother
Gabby, war buddy
Rom'n Rezalton, age 8
Horned Apparition (magic man)
Sacrificial Boy
Uppercadet's Voice
Grownup's Voice
MegaCorp Executive
2nd MegaCorp Executive
Narrator, poems
Boy on Transfer Shuttle
Sil'nov, Rom'n's friend
Man Behind Desk
Older Teen, during hazing
UnderGen'l V'jork
Announcer, tribunal
The Old Man, a CaptGen'l
Shr'dt, sector-lieute'nt
Crewmember, notifies Bofsky
Officer, protests blackmail
Braxtn, security chief
Robn't, Braxtn's assistant
Man at Desk
Freighter Tug Capt'n
Ben'frn
1st Voice
2nd Voice
3rd Voice
4th Voice
5th Voice
Dr.Sci. Refren Ascott
CityGov'r Reenson

WorldGov'r
1st Verification Team Member
2nd Verification Team Member
GlobalPresident Benetin
Magistrate
Visitor to Braxtn
Woman in Snow
Ens't, traitor
Sunsett, girlfriend
Answering Machine Voice (Ollen)
Dockworker
Tianne, Braxtn's wife
Braxtn, age 22
Cargo Handler
Woman in Bed
Nalt'n, Pack Grunt
Teammate on Se'Yan't
Alb't deFralin, sociologist
Aide to deFralin
Reconstruction Worker
Eight-Year-Old Boy on Shore
Colleague, shares with deFralin

ACT I - DECIMATION

INT. DARK ROOM - DAY (PRESENT)

The room is darkened. It is not pretty,
nor is it clean. RJORCK is visible, and
it is clear he has been confined in this
room for some time. Even in the darkness,
it is apparent he is very old and has been
beaten and tortured. He is backed into a
corner, seated. He gingerly caresses red
and raw wounds around his wrists.

Rjorck leans his head back against the
wall, looking up, extreme distress written
across his face. He slowly closes his
eyes.

MONTAGE:

Scenes are sharper than life. Brights are
very bright. Darks are very dark. Colors
are very washed out. In several of these
scenes, two suns are hanging in the sky,
one very large, and another smaller.

Mouths are speaking, telling of the old
myths of the power of the *poi'ntr'in*.

Flashes of people going into the sea, atrocities committed by MegaCorp, even snippets of Rjorck's own torture.

People walk fresh from the sea only to be roughly accosted, even killed by MegaCorp soldiers.

Finally, images of ADHOR'K, his beloved sister, now dead, in her strongest of moments, are seen.

BACK TO RJORCK:

Tears are running down Rjorck's face. Despair is in his eyes.

                    RJORCK
          (quietly, lips barely moving)
     Monsters. Monsters. I have
     only my *poi'ntr'in* to give.

Rjorck tucks his arms between his legs. He presses his feet firmly to the floor. He steels his face.

FLASHBACK (ONE DAY EARLIER):

INT. OPERATING THEATER – DAY

Rjorck is contorted with pain, his back arching. Behind him is MA'JENE HOLCUM dressed in the black uniform of a MegaCorp officer, the M C logo clearly emblazoned across her chest.

                    RJORCK
     Ahhhh!
          (ragged gasps of breath)

Rjorck, filthy and ragged, drops back to the table.

Rjorck's sweat-soaked head rolls to one side as his blood-shot eyes plead with his tormentor.

Holcum stands behind him with a NeuroShok stick in her hand.

> RJORCK
>
> I beg of you, UnderGen'l Holcum. There is no other secret. We swim in the seas; that is all. You have it on your VidPlay. You've shown me the clips again and again. What my people do is nothing else other than what you see.

> HOLCUM
>
> A full year we've been here! A wasted year! You do nothing in the sea except *disappear!* Where do you go? Why do only the old enter the sea to die, but we have plucked only the young as they emerge? I will know!

Holcum thumbs her NeuroShok stick, holding it toward Rjorck as the tip begins to sizzle.

> HOLCUM (CONT'D)
>
> Or have you begun to *enjoy* the pain . . .

INT.   LOOKING THROUGH INTERIOR WINDOW -
DAY

WILLANE BOFSKY is looking through the
window into the operating theater.

> BOFSKY
> She is quite good. I
> trained her myself, you
> know. Many people on many
> worlds have enjoyed the
> caress of her touch.

Bofsky reaches down to straighten his
sleeve cuff.

> BOFSKY (CONT'D)
> Although few of those ever
> will again.

> FIRST OFFICER
> But, Ser. No more have come
> from the sea for many days.
> This Rjorck is the last
> native alive. And we still
> don't know their secret.

Bofsky steps from the observation window.
It turns opaque as he does so. He reaches
to a locker door.

> BOFSKY
>   (growling)
> It wasn't about getting
> answers that I was referring
> to.

Bofsky opens the locker door with
unmistakable anticipation on his face, and
he picks up a NeuroShok stick.

ACT II - FLASHBACKS

INT.   LOCKER ROOM - DAY (FIFTEEN YEARS
EARLIER)

An open locker stands in a long row of
closed lockers. Suddenly the locker slams
with a hand held flat against the now
closed locker. Immediately, a much
younger Holcum, about fourteen years old,
slams herself backwards against the
locker. Her fist repeatedly slams the
locker at waist level.

            HOLCUM
      (hissing, mouth tight)
   A kid! He called me a kid!

INT.   AIR DUCT - DAY

Holcum and ROM'N REZALTON, a boy her age,
are crowded in a horizontal metal air
duct. The boy is dragging a bag with him.
It is very tight. Light leaks in from
vent openings on both sides. Holcum looks
pleased with reaching one vent in
particular.

                    HOLCUM
        Take this, Rezalton.
        Careful, you sloppy pig.

Holcum hands a detonator to Rezalton. He
takes it and puts it in his pocket.

                    HOLCUM (CONT'D)
        Get your arm off my leg, you
        idiot.
             (growling)
        If you can't help me do
        this, get your lazy tail
        back between your legs, and
        go play with yourself in
        your bunk like you did all
        night last night.

                    REZALTON
             (pleadingly)
        Don't tell, Ma'jene. The
        others. They'll think that
        - well, just don't tell,
        okay?

                    HOLCUM
        I will if you don't do what
        I ask, pretty boy. That
        pretty face of yours ain't
        good for *jack* right now. I
        need *smarts*.

Holcum flips up the vent screen and scoots
through the tight opening, dropping onto
her nemesis' bunk.

                    HOLCUM (CONT'D)
        He's going to regret what he
        did to me. And you're going
        to help me make sure he

does.

Holcum reaches back inside the vent and grabs Rezalton's arm, pulling him roughly into the room.

                    HOLCUM (CONT'D)
          Hand me the bag, kiddo.

Rezalton's eyes cut to the vent opening and back to Holcum.

                    REZALTON
          Still in the vent, Ma'jene.
          I'll get it. Hold on!

Rezalton leaps up to grab the bag out of the vent, and falls back on the bunk, the bag landing on top of his chest.

                    HOLCUM
          Stupid!

Holcum slaps Rezalton hard on the leg.

                    HOLCUM (CONT'D)
          That bag will take you out,
          and me along with it, if you
          set it off. You idiot! Be
          careful for a change.

Holcum reaches out and yanks the bag from Rezalton's chest.

                    REZALTON
               (with bravado)
          I can take you, Ma'jene.
          You know I can. I'm the
          best in all my activity-
          training levels. All the

girls like me. I'm number
two in all my classes, ahead
of even you. Quit picking
on me.

Rezalton rolls off the bunk, flexing his
arms to make his point.

                HOLCUM
            (sharply)
        Pansy. I need brains and a
        little self-control right
        now. Not your tos'rone.
        Keep your shirt on. You
        don't want all those girls
        to know about your private
        party last night.

                REZALTON
            (chastised)
        Sorry, Ma'jene. I'll be
        good. What do you need?

Rezalton reaches over and starts to unzip
the bag.

                REZALTON (CONT'D)
        What kind did you bring?
        LightCrackers? FizzPoppers?
        Any good ones?

Rezalton pulls one of the 'toys' from the
bag, holding it up to the light.

                REZALTON (CONT'D)
        Whoa! You're kidding?
        C'mon, Ma'jene. A
        BodyThumper? Hey, not even
        Overcadet Timons deserves
        this. Whatever he did to

you can't be *that* bad.
> (raises eyebrows)

Holcum yanks the explosive from Rezalton's
hand.

> HOLCUM
> (hisses)
> You don't know, don't
> understand. No one can.
> But pay. Yes, he'll pay.
> And you, Rezalton, you're in
> it with me. You and your
> pretty-boy looks, good at
> everything. We're a team
> now, you and me. So get
> with the program. You'll do
> as I say. Got it?

Holcum's eyes search the room for the best
hiding spot. Sweat begins to stain the
back of Rezalton's shirt as he takes the
explosive from Holcum and puts it back in
the bag.

> REZALTON
> (voice dead)
> Yeah, I got it, Ma'jene.
> We're a team. You and me.
> We're a team.
> (pulls detonator from pocket)
> How can I help you hook this
> up? What do you need me to
> do?

INT. OVERCADET TIMONS' QUARTERS - NIGHT

This is a clean, spare, well-lit cabin.
Every item is either stored or in its
place, the quarters of a fastidious

person. Centered is a door into the
corridor. To the right is a bathroom.
Right, unseen, is the bunk recessed into
the wall.

The door opens, and OVERCADET TIMONS walks
through the door. He unsnaps the collar
of his jacket, removing it and hanging it
in his storage locker. He pulls off his
shoes and pants, hanging the pants by the
creases.

He takes a can of polish from a recessed
drawer. Pulling a low bench out from the
wall on the left, he sits, wearing just
his undershirt and shorts, bringing his
shoes up to a regulation shine. He holds
them up to his face. He can see the
reflection of his own face in the polished
surface.

Timons sets the shoes in the locker under
the rest of his uniform and steps into the
bathroom. He leaves the door open. He
strips his remaining clothes off, dropping
them through a recessed recycle door.
Timons steps into his private shower
stall, still doorless, the steam billowing
around him. As he finishes, he reaches
for a towel from a dispenser on the wall,
dropping it into the same recycle slot
when finished.

Timons steps back into the room where he
seems to enjoy standing in the cool wash
of air from the vent. He yawns, then
walks to another drawer, pulling a fresh
pair of shorts and donning them. Timons
slips under the thin blanket on his bed.
As he stretches out to relax, suddenly the

scene erupts into an inferno as an explosion rips Overcadet Timons' bunk apart.

INT.   AWARDS CEREMONY - DAY

The entire academy student body is assembled. In the distance is a wide podium with several elaborately dressed officers and two undercadets.

The SQUAD COMMANDER begins to speak.

> SQUAD COMMANDER
> Congratulations, Undercadets Holcum and Rezalton. Due to your quick thinking and tenacious rescue efforts, what could have escalated into a section-wide disaster affecting the entire uppercadet class portion of the ship was restricted to three deaths, one from the actual, unexplained explosion on Deck 4, and two others from cadets caught in explosive decompression situations when their emergency survival suits could not be accessed quickly enough. You, Undercadet Holcum, along with your classmate, Undercadet Rezalton, were most fortunate to have been carrying your Class 1 Emergency Survival Suits back from maintenance at the precise moment of the

explosion. MegaCorp
Military Training Arm is
pleased to award both of you
with a two-stage advance,
bringing you from undercadet
status to uppercadet.
Congratulations, again, on a
job well done.

The squad commander removes the three-bar
undercadet pin from each undercadet's
jacket. The commander takes two fitted
overcadet jackets, handing one to each of
the two teenagers. Holcum and Rezalton
don the jackets, waiting while the
commander pins new five-bar pins on each
lapel. The different classes all across
the scene, one class at a time, stand
clapping and cheering until all the
trainees are on their feet.

INT. ANTEROOM - DAY (MANY YEARS AND
LIFETIMES EARLIER)

RJORCK is seated at a table. A closed
doorway is across from him. He is about
eighteen or twenty, much younger than when
seen last time. He is handling the items
on the table, obviously waiting. Behind
him are portions of space suits, the type
worn by travelers in a spacecraft. They
look very out of place in the room. The
items Rjorck is handling are obviously
from a spacecraft, and he looks at them
longingly.

MONTAGE:

A series of scenes shows what has happened
since the spacecraft's arrival. In the

final few scenes, a VOICE OVER is heard.

The scenes include Rjorck seeing the
spacecraft land.

Rjorck learns to communicate with the men.

The men are shown much of the near-by
countryside.

A tour of a lacy, fairytale city is given.

There is a sequestered discussion among a
number of this world's elders.

> FIRST VOICE (VOICE OVER)
> These people bring much
> power with them.

> SECOND VOICE (VOICE OVER)
> We can never let them know
> of our renewal in our seas.
> They will try to take it.
> We have seen the food
> animals die. They fight for
> life so. These men will do
> the same.

> FIRST VOICE (VOICE OVER)
> We must choose a volunteer
> to be trained. To go to
> this Earth to look out for
> our interests. We must
> protect that which we are
> unable to share. These
> people will certainly try to
> take it if they learn our
> way. We have heard the
> stories of their worlds. We
> know the cruelties that

would happen to us.

            THIRD VOICE (VOICE OVER)
    We must convince one of
    theirs to stay with us so
    there will be room upon this
    ship's return to this Earth.

            FIRST VOICE (VOICE OVER)
    Easily done. Leave it to me.

BACK TO RJORCK:

The doorway across from Rjorck opens.
Rjorck's face jumps to a look of
hopefulness at the sound of the door.

The men from the previous montage enter
through the doorway. Rjorck is still
seated at the table, holding one of the
items from the spacecraft in his hands.
The men carry sadness on their faces as if
their decision is a condemnation. As one,
they nod yes. Rjorck jumps up from the
table with enthusiasm, his excitement at
the news seeming to mystify the men.

INT. SPACESHIP - DAY

A long corridor is seen. Along one side
is a series of twelve stacked bunks.
Rjorck walks into the scene. With
direction from one of the crew, Rjorck
places a small bundle inside a storage
container next to one of the bunks. The
crewmember instructs Rjorck how to open
the bunk. A glassine door retracts.
Rjorck slips inside.

Rjorck is lying in the bunk. It is very

tight. As Rjorck looks out and smiles at
the now unseen crewmember, the glass
closes. The interior fills with an opaque
gas.

INT. SPACESHIP - DAY (MONTHS LATER)

This is the same long corridor as in the
previous scene. Along one side is the
same series of twelve stacked bunks. All
the glassine bunk doors are closed except
one on the far end. The lighting is on in
the corridor but turned down low, little
more than a glow. A soft light radiates
from inside each of the stacked bunks
adding additional light to the scene.

Rjorck is lying in one of the bunks,
obscured by the previously seen opaque
gas. There is a visible shift in the gas
as much of it is immediately dissipated.
Obviously, it has been some time since he
entered the bunk. His face is heavy with
beard, and his hair is somewhat longer
than when he entered the bunk. The sound
of a hand is heard slapping the controls
by his bunk, the sharp release of an air
pressure seal makes Rjorck jerk, and the
glassine starts to move.

A crewmember moves rapidly down the
corridor, slapping a large red release
panel beside each bunk. As he slaps each
remaining panel, the panel turns orange,
then green as the glassine doors rise. As
they do, one after another, the cold steam
slides into the corridor, joining with the
cloud gathering from the bunks down the
wall. The brightness of regular corridor
lighting flickers on. Brilliant lighting

flickers on in the bunks, one here, then three, one of the bunks flickering on, then off, then back on to full brightness.

Groans and voiced comments are heard from various people:

> 1st PERSON (OFF SCREEN)
> (groaning)
> Shiking deep sleep!

> 2nd PERSON (OFF SCREEN)
> Welcome home, honey!

> 3rd PERSON (OFF SCREEN)
> (sour laughter)
> The blessings of MegaCorp
> travel service are at your
> disposal!

> 4th PERSON (OFF SCREEN)
> Can I get some water here?

> 2nd PERSON (OFF SCREEN)
> Gods, my head hurts!

> 1st PERSON (OFF SCREEN)
> (urgently)
> Pouch here, stat!

Rjorck opens his eyes, and intense discomfort is seen on his face. He shifts and groans, licking his lips, working his mouth as if full of cotton. He arches his neck as if to relieve the discomfort, and his eyes squeeze tightly shut. An unseen crew member's hand roughly slaps a pouch on Rjorck's chest. Rjorck reflexively grabs the package with his own hand, holding it right where the crewmember placed it.

                    CREWMEMBER
        Here! Nourishment. You'll
        feel better when you get
        this down. It's always
        worse the first time.
        Welcome to interstellar
        space travel. Not all it's
        knocked up to be. Drink!

The voice of the crewmember trails off
down the corridor, soon heard again as
another of the crew is encouraged to
consume the contents of the pouch.

Rjorck puts the pouch to his mouth, and
his facial features relax. He lays his
head back, his eyes closing in relief.

EXT. SPACEPORT ON EARTH - DAY

Buildings are placed around the scene.
There are flying craft of all kinds,
shapes, and sizes. This is an orderly
place, but much as would be seen around
the business end of a modern-day airport
terminal, often-used items are placed here
and there, set aside for convenience,
ready for immediate reuse. The buildings
are relatively low with heavy glassine
walls allowing visitors to look inside.
The landing areas are pitted and blackened
as if having endured many decades and even
centuries of use.

One ship is already opened. Several
people, crew and ground crew, are moving
occasionally in and out. Rjorck, his
small parcel of personal items in his

hand, descends, turning his face to soak
up the warmth from Earth's single sun.

Rjorck closes his eyes, soaking up the
warmth, enjoying himself very much. A
hand slaps Rjorck on the shoulder.
Surprised, Rjorck starts, looking at the
man, giving him his attention. It is the
crewmember that helped Rjorck into his
bunk on the ship.

The crewmember is walking backwards, a
satchel in his hand, wearing casual
civvies, pants, a rough pocketed shirt,
and worn leather shoes. He grins as he
raises his hand and motions for Rjorck to
follow him.

INT. HALLWAY - DAY

RJORCK is looking down, fiddling with
something unfamiliar. He is inside a
corridor, standing before a door, trying
to work the opening mechanism. Directly
in front of Rjorck's face is a sign that
can be clearly read as Rjorck works on the
lock.

EF'NCY UNIT 917F. WELCOME TO YOUR FREE
LODGINGS. STAY AS LONG AS YOU LIKE.

In smaller letters underneath are the
additional words,

CONFORMS TO CODE 10.2398-JH098,
INTERPLANET RESIDENCY STANDARDS.

After a few moments, Rjorck finally
releases the door, opening it.

Rjorck enters a small room with a built-in desk and data access terminal (a.k.a. *computer* to us, *glass* to the characters) to the left, a built-in bed recessed into the wall directly ahead, and a wall of storage to the right. Unseen to the far left, a small corridor juts off to the bathroom door. Rjorck lays his own small parcel on the bunk and immediately sits down to the terminal. He reaches out to touch the glass, the word TUTORIAL coming up on the display.

Rjorck's hands reach out and begin manipulating simple 3-D geometric shapes of different colors on the glass. Words scroll quickly across the glass' surface. No more do the words appear than Rjorck's hands snap to one of the shapes, the words fading out as Rjorck performs the required tutorial task.

Rjorck continues at this for a minute, very quickly moving, twisting, pulling, and pushing the shapes in many different ways. Suddenly, they all fade with the following words appearing on the screen. THANK YOU. TUTORIAL COMPLETE. YOU MAY BEGIN. These letters fade as a talking news channel tumbles onto the glass from the left side. Much as with news channels on the modern-day Internet, there are moving pictures, columns of information, and many choices. The columns are continually scrolling, the talking head sliding from column to column. Rjorck moves his fingers toward the screen, and as he moves his hands, columns grow, shift, and shrink. He pulls a talking head out, the voice growing louder, then

pushes it back to the background as it
quiets down, all the while never touching
the screen. Rjorck flicks his fingers,
and the entire contents of the screen
break into individual boxes, tumbling over
each other off the edge of the glass, a
new screen of information tumbling in from
the other side. As he works, a pattern
emerges on the data unit. He is accessing
banking and financial information.

INT. BANKING INSTITUTION - DAY

Rjorck is sitting in a chair in a banking
institution. A well-dressed BANKER sits
at a desk just across from Rjorck. A
glass is suspended above the banker's
desk, and he is manipulating the unseen
information much as Rjorck did in the
previous scene. A smile grows on the
banker's face as he pulls information from
his terminal, his hands moving faster and
faster. He stands, steps around his desk,
turns to Rjorck, and holds out a hand to
congratulate Rjorck. He seems quite
impressed and very deferential as he
smiles and begins to speak.

                    BANKER
        I hadn't realized you were
        so well placed in so many
        corporations. Your history
        of long-standing accounts is
        quite extensive. I wouldn't
        have expected one so
        youthful to be so
        accomplished. I must admit,
        I am impressed, Ser Rjorck.

Rjorck shows a forgiving smile, shaking

the banker's hand.

                    RJORCK
          As I said, just check the
          information on my record
          stick. My transaction
          history is very commendable.
          Just a small loan will do.
          Perhaps eighty thousand
          credits repayable in ninety
          days.

                    BANKER
          We can provide you much
          more, Ser. Rjorck. Are you
          sure eighty thousand will be
          enough?

                    RJORCK
          That is kind of you.
          However, I'm sure the eighty
          thousand will be sufficient.

                    BANKER
          Do you have a credit stick
          with you? If not, I'm sure
          we can provide you with one.

                    RJORCK
          Yes, that would be nice.
             (rising to exit)
          May I pick it up at the front desk?

                    BANKER
          I will see that it is
          waiting on you, Ser Rjorck.
          Please, do come again. My
          personal business
          information will be encoded
          directly onto your new

credit stick.   Contact me at
any time.

Rjorck rises to leave as the banker turns
his attention back to his work.

Rjorck holds his arm in front of his chest
as he grins and clenches his fist in a
victory clench.

INT. 'GLASS' DATA TERMINAL - NIGHT (THIRTY
YEARS LATER)

RJORCK's hands are once again manipulating
information on a data terminal 'glass.'
These hands are older than the young man's
hands seen in the previous scene. As
information is pulled forward, Rjorck's
name can be clearly seen. The account
balances are staggering. The hands pull
up news reports with Rjorck's name
connected to important world events, even
the name Rejuvenant, his homeworld. Then
he accesses accounts of a darker nature.
Weapons shipments, political intrigue, and
blackmail.

This is a firmly middle-aged Rjorck, his
clothing and surroundings evidently very
prosperous. We hear him murmur to
himself.

                    RJORCK
          Oh, the machinations I've
          instigated to protect my
          precious Se'Yan't.
              (pause, then almost under his
              breath)
          Whatever it takes. Whatever
          it takes.

                      36

For a few minutes, Rjorck continues to work the computer, occasionally writing on his desktop with a stylus, the words appearing on the 'glass' unit, tapping the stylus against the glass, placing the end of the stylus to his forehead or on his lips, then writing some more. There is every evidence that he has become a very important and busy man.

INT. MEGACORP ACADEMY TRAINING SHIP - DAY

MONTAGE:

Various scenes are seen, long shots of corridors, shower rooms, groups of cadets eating at tables or huddled over 'glass' data units, gathered, and all seem to be intently discussing some riveting news.

INT. COMMUNAL SHOWER ROOM - DAY

ROM'N REZALTON is a year younger than when seen last, although still taller than those around him and developed into quite a handsome youth. He is in the shower, and there is no door or curtain. Steam surrounds him. The sound of the running water is quite evident. Rezalton shows his profile, rinsing his hair, his arms above his head, and his face away from the water. A row of showers lines the two visible walls. There are no doors on these showers, either. In the center of the room is a series of low benches for the use of bathers as they dress and undress. A group of cadets is heard before they enter the room. Rezalton calls out before opening his eyes to look around.   He is still rinsing his hair.

> REZALTON
> Guys!

Sweaty boys of about fourteen years old
fill the room, talking excitedly, and one
reaches in to poke Rezalton as he walks
by. The boy turns to another boy after
doing so and points, laughing. By the
boys' attire, they appear to have come
from a physical activities class.

> REZALTON (CONT'D)
> It's Rom'n. Come talk to
> me. What's the big news
> going around?

Rezalton peers out through the steam. One
of the other boys, FIRST UNDERCADET, walks
up to the bench just in front of
Rezalton's shower.

> FIRST UNDERCADET
> Hey, Rom'n.

First Undercadet pulls his shirts and
shorts off, standing just in undershorts,
and he drops his clothing on the bench.

> FIRST UNDERCADET (CONT'D)
> New student on ship.

The other boys are also undressing,
kicking their clothes around, several of
them reaching inside empty shower cubicles
to turn on the water, then reaching up to
test the temperature.

                    REZALTON
          Nah, can't be.

Rezalton turns, standing in the shower
door, leaning forward on hands held
against the door opening.

                    REZALTON (CONT'D)
          No more newbies until a year
          from now. No exceptions.
          MegaCorp policy. You guys
          know that. Pull my leg
          again, and I'll come out of
          this shower and take you
          down, one at a time.
               (with bravado)
          Maybe I'll even stuff you in
          the showers, clothes on, all
          at the same time.

The other boys laugh nervously. Most of
them are smaller than Rezalton, and they
seem wary of his threat. In a sudden
flurry of activity, the other boys quickly
strip their clothing, tossing it to the
side, and dive into open showers. One
boy, LE'RANE, is nervously waiting, with
all the showers filled.

Another boy, SECOND UNDERCADET, is already
in his shower, but he has yet to turn on
the water. He flips the water on, jumping
out of the way as it spits cold water for
a second. He leans to look out of his
shower at Rezalton who's still standing in
the shower door.

                    SECOND UNDERCADET
          Tough luck there, Rom'n.
               (laughter)

                       39

Several of the boys lean out when the
laughter is heard. One flips water
Rezalton's direction. Another waves him
off with his hand. All laugh, and the
relieved expressions on their faces
suggest they are perhaps relieved to still
be on Rezalton's good side.

> THIRD UNDERCADET
> We're already in.

Steam billows out, making the boys look
like ghosts.

> THIRD UNDERCADET (CONT'D)
> Besides, it's really true.
> This one's an inductee,
> snatched from a converted
> world. The training
> commanders have been told
> they have to find room.

> REZALTON
> Gods!

Rezalton's eyes flick back and forth from
the towel dispenser to the bench and his
clothing. He seems to be reaching a
conclusion and making a decision.

> REZALTON (CONT'D)
> There's only one spot
> available, and I know where
> it is. Jeenky sticks!

Rezalton pirouettes out of the shower
doorway throwing water around the room.
He feints around the undercadet waiting
just outside his shower, slides to the

bench holding his shorts, grabs them in
one hand, and calls to the boy jumping out
of his way.

                    REZALTON (CONT'D)
          Shower's yours, Le'rane.

Le'rane replies over Rezalton's flurry of
activity.

                    LE'RANE
          I appreciate it, Rom'n.
          It's nice for you to leave
          my shower all warmed up.

INT.   CORRIDOR - DAY

Water is dripping from Rezalton's flushed
limbs as he sprints from the communal
shower room into the corridor, dodging
laughing cadets of all ratings, holding
his shorts in one hand, slipping down the
hall, using his free hand to push people
out of the way.

INT.   CO-ED DORM ROOM - DAY

Rezalton bursts into the dormitory, water
still dripping from his body, dancing as
he attempts to put his shorts on and run
at the same time. Breathing hard,
Rezalton slides up to his bunk. The other
bunks in the room are filled with boys and
girls Rezalton's age. Several of the
unoccupied bunks are unmade or filled with
items that fourteen-year-olds like to have
out. The bunk below his is the only one
in the room that is neatly made and
appears unused. However, there is a
duffel on it.

Rezalton puts his hands on his knees, panting, as he peers at the unknown duffel on the bottom bunk. He reaches to run his hand over two tags on the end of the bunks. The tag on the top has the name SIL'NOV clearly labeled. In red letters over the word is printed DECEASED. The tag on the bottom says REZALTON. Rezalton stands, twirling 180 degrees. He raises both arms, putting his fists to his forehead, closing his eyes in a grimace. His skin is very flushed. In one single, apparently practiced motion, he flips himself up on the top bunk, flipping both arms above his head as he lies back. Drops of water still dot his skin, and an intense look of resentful anger is on his face.

LATER:

Rezalton is on his stomach now, apparently asleep. A hand, obviously a girl's, reaches up to him. The girl, MA'JENE HOLCUM, age fourteen, pushes at Rezalton, two fingers on his shorts, and two on his skin. Rezalton's body rocks as the hand pushes him three times.

          HOLCUM
Hey! Pansy!

Rezalton's eyes open but seem unable to focus at first, as if he is being pulled from a very intense dream.

          HOLCUM (CONT'D)
You gonna greet me or just
lie there? You snooze, you

lose! Your loss!

Rezalton shakes his head to wake himself.
He pulls himself to the edge of the bed to
see the new undercadet below him. On his
face the resentful anger is returning with
the wakefulness. He leans his head over
and his eyes catch Holcum sitting on the
bunk below him. She is well-developed for
fourteen.

Once he gets a good look, Rezalton jerks
back on his bunk, his eyes wide. Holcum
stands and rests her arms on the edge of
Rezalton's bunk. She looks him over,
finally resting her eyes on his face.

          HOLCUM
Welcome to the real world,
jack! Err, what's the name?

          REZALTON
   (broken voice, clearing throat)
Rom'n.

          HOLCUM
   (amused)
Yeah, that's right, jack.
Rom'n. Well, you're a
pansy, Rom'n. Did anyone
ever tell you that? A real
pansy. A shiking good-
looking pansy, but still a
pansy. By the way, I'm
Ma'jene. All my friends
call me Ma'jene. At least
the ones who want to stay my
friends. Before you ask,
yeah, I'm a year late
gettin' here. A year late,

and a credit short.
Whatever. I'll just have to
hustle a little harder,
won't I? Anyway, I know one
thing for sure, I'm gonna
whup-up on that finely-
muscled backside all the
girls have been telling me
about.

Holcum grabs Rezalton's arm, pushes him
down on the sleeping mat, and plants a
slap firmly on his buttocks. Holcum
returns to busy herself on her bunk.

Rezalton flips effortlessly onto his back,
and in one motion, slips his hands under
his head. A grin settles on his features
as he closes his eyes.

INT. HOLCUM'S CHILDHOOD HOME - DAY (SIX
YEARS EARLIER)

The thumping of mortar explosions, many
distant, others sounding very close,
overshadow the sounds inside what is left
of Holcum's home. Much of the walls are
blown away. The roof and ceiling are
gone. The sky beyond is smoke-filled,
creating dimness in the scene. In one
dark corner is a GIRL about seven or
eight, clearly recognizable as a younger
version of Holcum from the last scene.
From behind a leather armchair, someone's
arm is lying on the floor as if reaching
for the girl. There is no one attached to
the arm. The girl whimpers and reaches
for the dismembered arm, anyway. There is
a resounding boom nearby indicating a
large explosion. The girl yanks her arm

back into her protective huddle.
Suddenly, a bright light held by an UNSEEN
SOLDIER flashes in the girl's face.

>   1st SOLDIER
>   We've got a live one!
>   Quick, before this one gets
>   away!

A scuffle of sound and of boards and other
household items being kicked out of the
way and or thrown aside tell us the girl
is being cornered.

Suddenly, several black-suited figures
appear out of the dust and darkness.

The girl's eyes cut between what is left
of her parents and the black-suited
figures. The girl explosively shoots
through the remains of her home. She runs
down a hallway and through what is left of
an exterior doorway, and the darkness she
runs into resolves itself into a black-
suited SECOND SOLDIER that grabs her.

>   2nd SOLDIER
>   Got her!

The girl struggles unsuccessfully to
escape the soldier's hold.

INT. MOVING CONTAINER - DAY

Little is visible. The sheen of a
metallic blackness flickers. The scene
jumps with irregularity indicating being
carried in a container over bomb damaged
roads. After a few minutes of this . . .

MONTAGE:

Flashes of what must be memories are seen,
softened and slightly askew, the edges
fuzzy, jerking in the same pattern as at
the beginning of the scene. Flashes of
home. Loving arms wrapped around her.
Kisses. Warmth. Bright sun. Happy
sounds. Colors flashing by. Music. And
interspersed, darkness. Bumps.

BACK TO MOVING CONTAINER:

Barely visible in the darkness, the girl
explores the blackness of her prison with
slender fingers, finally finding a crack.
She works the crack, finding the latch.
Her fingers force their way in and an
audible click is heard. A vertical strip
of light appears. She pushes and sees a
nightmarish scene. No trees. No blue
sky. No one she knows. No home. Smoke.
Dark-suited figures. Fallen buildings.
Sadness.

Dirty, soot covered, and clearly turning
feral with shock and desperation, the
girl's eyes flick through all she sees,
making the hard choices.

EXT. MOVING CONTAINER - DAY

The metal container the girl has been
riding in is being pulled in a train of
similar boxes. The door of the girl's box
opens a fraction. Suddenly it is pushed
wide by a small arm. The girl jumps and
runs from the moving transport. The girl
disappears among the wreckage of
buildings.

EXT.   SCENE OF DESTRUCTION - DAY

The girl is running through bomb-damaged
structures, small in the larger view of
her world's destruction, her story a small
event against a much larger attack on her
world.   Her world now consists of flaming
debris, attacking ships, and lasers
lancing through smoke filled skies.   The
sounds of all this rise to cover the
sounds of her escape.

ACT III — THE ARRIVAL

EXT.   ROCKY PROMONTORY ON
REJUVENANT/SE'YAN'T — DAY

RJORCK is obviously freshly reborn,
looking to be about eighteen or twenty.
He stands on the edge of a rocky
promontory, the ground dropping away at
his feet.   The brilliant day stretches
away in the distance and the beauty of a
verdant rift valley far below is
mesmerizing.   In the extreme distance is
the ever-blue sea of this world.   Above is
Rejuvenant/Se'Yan't's ever-present yellow
sky.   Her twin suns are overhead, one
smaller, and the other very large.

Rjorck is standing looking away from his
FRIENDS, his hair thick with waves and
long from a year of growth in the seas.
He is wearing long robes, weighted and
tied for propriety.   He turns, looking at
the group.   E'VONN, youthful, his face
filled with humor, is barely visible as he
turns for a moment to catch Rjorck's eye
then shifts his attention back to the
group of friends.

                    RJORCK
                (emphatically)
          It was, too. Come with me
          during the next 'little
          night' and you will see. It
          was there. I saw it, and so
          did Adhor'k and Berian.
          They were there. They saw
          it, too, with their own
          eyes. It was brighter than
          last time, too.
                (stamps foot)

                    E'VONN
                (teasingly)
          Rjorck. You surely left the
          better part of your
          hyr'yan't in the sea!

There is warm laughter from the group of
friends.

EXT. PICNIC ON PROMONTORY - SAME DAY

Rjorck is still facing away from his
friends, looking out to the view off the
promontory. The sky is different, the
shadows longer. His friends are seated
behind him. They are enjoying each
other's company, and food is spread out on
a mat, places set for each of the
participants. One place is empty,
Rjorck's. He stands for a long time, very
youthful, the stiff breeze blowing his
hair back from his face, and the softness
of the two setting suns warming his skin.
His friends continue their meal,
occasionally calling out to him, and the
yellow sky behind him softens from a
brilliant yellow to a softer gold.

EXT. ROCKY BEACH - DAY (SEVERAL DAYS
LATER)

The twin suns are high in the yellow sky,
one larger than the other. Centered
between them is the flaring of a rocket's
exhaust pulsing, growing rapidly closer.
The brilliance of the exhaust dwarfs even
the twin suns' brilliance. It is quickly
roaring and growing louder.

The ship lands, and the stone-covered
shore is clearly seen in the distance. A
number of people are crouching behind
large stones in the deep shadows produced
by the flaring of the exhaust. Rjorck is
seen out in the open, refusing to hide in
the shadows. He holds his ears and fights
against the blast of the craft's landing.
Suddenly, the craft has landed, and the
brilliance and sound are gone. In the
silence, the twin shadows return, and the
lapping of the sea's waters can be heard.
The others seem unsure and frightened with
only Rjorck standing erect and fascinated.
He has an elegant profile, his youth not
disguising the determined set of curiosity
on his face. He has the stance of a man
who wants to know more.

There is a screeching sound as the side of
the craft splits open, clattering to the
rocky ground. The startled observers step
back when the clattering is heard. Twelve
SPACE-SUITED HUMANS walk from the ship,
looking around in curiosity and amazement.

Rjorck moves forward even as his peers
move back to their hiding places. He

stands tall as he delivers a formal
greeting.

                    RJORCK
                 (brazenly)
          Welcome travelers. You must
          have journeyed far to speak
          with us. What manner of
          vessel is this to have flown
          through our skies, to have
          wrestled courageously with
          our twin suns, and moved
          with an intensity more
          brilliant than our brightest
          day?

One of the space-suited men presses a hand
to his neck. An audible click is heard as
the top of his suit collapses with a
whirring sound to form a wide collar. The
man takes a deep breath, and a smile grows
on his face as he motions for his
companions to also release their helmets.

The space-suited men walk excitedly up to
the waiting Rjorck, the first man offering
a suited hand to Rjorck in greeting.

ACT IV - THE REASON FOR BOFSKY

INT.   COUNSELOR'S OFFICE - DAY

A boy about twelve, 'Willy' Willane
Bofsky, is sitting in a chair, his arms
crossed, a look of defiance on his face.

A man, a COUNSELOR, stands behind a window
looking in at the boy. The man picks up a
type of thumb drive, a data stick,
slipping it into a data terminal known as
a 'glass.'

The counselor visibly sighs, reaching his
hand up to scroll through the information
on the glass panel in front of him. The
following information is seen: WILLANE
BARD BOFSKY. NO KIN. SIGNS OF PHYSICAL
ABUSE. FOUND SEVERELY BEATEN.

The man reaches up and uses two fingers to
grab a set of new words, bringing them
forward. Then we catch the following:
FIGHTING, ABUSIVE, BROUGHT BLOOD,
BELLIGERENT, DESTRUCTIVE.

The counselor steps over to a door leading
into the other room where the boy sits.

As he places his hand on the pressure
plate that will read his palm signature,
the man pauses and shakes his head in a
hopeless manner. His hand presses down,
the door swings open, and he steps through
the opening door.

                    COUNSELOR
          Willane. Or do you prefer
          Willy?

Bofsky growls, and he flicks his eyes at
the man and back away again.

                    BOFSKY
          Willy's for babies. Don't
          call me that.

                    COUNSELOR
          What happened this morning,
          Willane?
               (raises eyebrows)

                    BOFSKY
          Keep those others away from
          my bunk, that's what
          happened. Get too close
          again, I'll teach 'em.
          Break a finger, maybe.
               (pauses expectantly, glaring)
          Maybe their nose. I know
          how.

                    COUNSELOR
          You do know one of the boys
          is in the medcenter. You
          put him there. Do you think
          he deserved that?

                    BOFSKY
I told him. Leave my stuff
alone. He didn't. He put
himself in the medcenter.
Sure seems that way to me.
Did it to himself.

                    COUNSELOR
He broke his own foot?
Explain that little angle to
me.

                    BOFSKY
Didn't say he broke it. I
broke it. Clean. He caused
it, though. Consequences.
You do stupid, stuff
happens. He did stupid. I
happened to him. That's the
way life works. At least
that's the way my life
works.

                    COUNSELOR
What about the pain you must
have caused for him? Did
you think about your action
regarding his pain? What
about the inconvenience of
being stuck in the
medcenter, not able to walk?

                    BOFSKY
Pain! One little foot. He
doesn't know pain. He ran
away, didn't he? His foot
couldn't have been *too*
broken.
     (shifting, bored)
Hey. Don't you have some

bad students here, worse
than me? Like murderers or
rapists? Come on, it was
just his foot.

                    COUNSELOR
Willane, you're proving a
danger to students your own
age and size. This has not
been the first report of
aggression toward others in
your housing block. The
decision has been reached to
transfer you to the
fourteen/fifteen block.

                    BOFSKY
            (interrupting)
Hrmp! That's got me so
scared. They'll keep me in
line, huh? Well, you'd
better tell them just to
keep away. And those
others, they'll get what's
coming to them. Just see.
You'll see.
            (disdain dripping from his voice)
There are other ways to get
them. So, you tell them.
Leave me alone. Don't mess
with me unless they want me
to mess back.

                    COUNSELOR
What do you mean by that,
Willane?

                    BOFSKY
Nothing. Just, you'll see.

Bofsky leans back, crossing determined arms across his chest.

> COUNSELOR
> (attempt at sincerity)
> I really do want you to do well here at Public Academy, Bel'age. All the staff want that for you. However, this is a two-way street. Right now you're on a one-way street going the wrong way. You've still got a chance to fix this.
> (pause)
> You may go, Willane. A good first step in starting over would be to stop by the medcenter to see the boy with the broken foot.

> BOFSKY
> (with attitude)
> Yeah. Whatever. Whatever you want.

Bofsky stands and exits the room. He stands in the corridor outside the counselor's office. Behind him, through the glass wall, the counselor glances at Bofsky, shakes his head, and turns to his desk, sitting. As Bofsky storms past, he finishes the words he did not say to the counselor.

> BOFSKY
> (terse, through teeth)
> Tell my mother there's still time to fix it, time to start over. There is no

starting over.

INT. BOFSKY'S BUNK - DAY

Bofsky is packing his storage locker. He keeps a small box out. He grins as he opens the box.

            BOFSKY
        (intensely)
     Don't mess with Willane,
     'cause Willane messes back.

INT. 12/13-YEAR-OLD DORM - DAY

Bofsky is walking though the dorm stopping to do something at every bunk. At each bunk, he takes out a razor blade, slices a slit in the seam of the mattress, and slips the razor blade inside, the cutting edge carefully pointing up. Then, he straightens the covers to make the bed appear undisturbed. Each time this happens, Bofsky repeats himself.

            BOFSKY
     Don't mess with Willane,
     'cause Willane messes back.

INT. COUNSELOR AT HIS DESK - DAY

The same counselor as in the previous scene is sitting at his desk. He picks up a corded listening device and hits a button on it. He appears to smirk as he speaks into the device.

            COUNSELOR
     Counselor Renan? I have a
     twelve/thirteen I'm sending

up. He's a charity ward who
thinks he's a bit tougher
than the other guys. I'd
like you to get some of your
bigger fifteens to cut him
down to size.
     (pauses)
A little blood wouldn't
hurt. No, it wouldn't hurt
at all.

INT. BOFSKY'S BUNK - NIGHT

Bofsky is lying in his bunk. Lighting
comes from the odd undercounter lighting,
outside corridor lighting, some street
lighting seen through painted-over
windows, and from exit signs. Bofsky's
eyes are open and alert. He is lying very
still as the noise of someone moving
around is heard. Bofsky starts and then
freezes.

          BOFSKY
     (whispering)
Who's there?
     (jumps when he hears an answer)

          1st 14/15-YEAR-OLD
     (deep voice, quietly)
So, you are awake. That's
better than you being
asleep. We might've had to
keep you quiet - not fun for
anyone, us or you. We don't
want anyone else to know
where you're going on
vacation for tonight.

Multiple hands reach, pulling Bofsky to

his feet, throwing his covers aside.
Bofsky seems to be very focused and intent
as if noticing every detail.

                1st 14/15-YEAR-OLD
         We're going to become very
         good friends, tonight. Yep,
         the best of friends.
            (snickers)
         No noise from you, now.
         Noise is bad and will make
         your vacation worse. Just
         come with us.

One boy leans to whisper in Bofsky's ear
as a blindfold is tied around Bofsky's
eyes.

                2nd 14/15-YEAR-OLD
            (cruelly)
         The face is off-limits. We
         won't bother *that,* but the
         face isn't the interesting
         part, anyway. The rest of
         you belongs to us for the
         duration of your vacation.
         Welcome to the world of the
         big boys, little twelve-
         thirteen.

                3rd 14/15-YEAR-OLD
            (with disgust)
         Phew! The baby just peed
         his shorts!

INT.   SCHOOL'S COMMUNAL SHOWERS - NIGHT

These showers are very similar to those
seen on board the MegaCorp academy vessel,
but these are obviously ground-based and

very well used. They have open shower
doors, dingy white tile, and suspended
wire lighting. These showers have seen
better days.

Several older-looking boys are standing,
showing their full height and musculature.
All are wiry. All the boys are wearing
the standard issue disposable shorts just
as Bofsky is. This is not an institution
where students are especially well clothed
or well fed. In the center is Bofsky,
blindfolded, wearing just his undershorts.

>   2nd 14/15-YEAR-OLD
> Can you tell where we are,
> little man? You know this
> place. You've been here
> before. Just yesterday we
> watched you take off all
> your clothes, stand in the
> water getting all wet, then
> put your clothes back on.
> We're around you all the
> time. That trick you played
> with the mattresses? Some
> of those kids are our
> friends. You shouldn't have
> done that.

Bofsky breathes very quickly and loudly.

>   2nd 14/15-YEAR-OLD
> We'll always know you, but
> you'll never know who we
> are. Watch it.

Bofsky gasps and jerks as the older boys
begin kicking him. Bofsky falls to the
floor, blood smearing the tile under him.

                    BOFSKY
               (desperately)
          Stop!

The older boys pick up Bofsky and carry
him to one of the showers. They hold him
for a minute as one of the boys reaches in
and flips on the water. The water spits
loudly, and it spatters unevenly, finally
settling to a haphazard if strong spray.

Bofsky is held up with his feet on the
floor, and the blindfold is still on.
Bofsky's face is clean, but blood is
seeping from multiple places on his chest,
stomach, and arms. A new boy speaks.

                4th 14/15-YEAR-OLD
          A cold shower might be just
          the thing to cool your
          heels. Everyone knows your
          stunt from the
          twelve/thirteens. Some of
          them are our friends, and
          you hurt them for no reason.
          Stupid, stupid, stupid,
          little man, and I do mean
          little man, you are not
          smart. Remember, we know
          you.

The older boys toss Bofsky, leaving him
lying askew in the shower. He is sitting,
leaning to his right, his knees raised in
front of him, his right arm stretched out
along the shower floor. His left arm is
across his lap.

Water spatters over Bofsky. His skin is

                       61

covered in chill bumps, and it
involuntarily shivers. Blood runs down
the drain.

INT. EMPTY HALLWAY - DAY

The hallway stretches with numerous doors
widely spaced. This is obviously a very
old, poorly maintained building. Bofsky
steps out of one doorway, looking back and
forth, constantly alert. He is neatly
dressed for class. When he starts down
the hallway, he lurches and dashes as
quickly as he can, constantly looking all
the while.

INT. CLASSROOM - DAY

The class is in session with the teacher
talking. This is a science lab, one that
might be found on any world in any
century. At this school, it might well
have been built two hundred years ago.
Numerous boys of middle teen years are
sitting at stools at tall tables across
the room. The classroom has two doors
with glass windows. At one of the doors
is Bofsky's face peering in, his eyes
cutting across the bank of students.

Bofsky opens the door, looking very
carefully at available seats as if
cautious about who might be near him. He
gently closes the door, as if trying to
sneak in unobserved.

                    TEACHER
            (with real warmth)
        Ah! I've been waiting,
        Willane. This is your first

day of class with us.

Bofsky freezes when the teacher speaks
directly to him.

> TEACHER (CONT'D)
> (with encouragement)
> Welcome to the new session.
> I didn't want to assign
> groups until you showed up.
> This will be a lab class, so
> many activities will be
> partnered. Also, I would
> like everyone to notice the
> exceptional age range of the
> students. Many of you are
> seeing students with whom
> you've never been in class
> before. Get to know one
> another. Older students
> will be paired with younger
> students as much as
> practicality allows. No
> belittling. No whining.
> Let's get started.

Bofsky looks and sees no one paying him
any attention. As Bofsky notices the
other students ignoring him, he moves to
the closest seat he can find.

> TEACHER
> (suddenly)
> Bofsky, you and Gr'gan pair up.

Bofsky starts, glancing around in a panic.
He settles down when he sees a smiling
face, GR'GAN RHNST, wave at him.

                    TEACHER (CONT'D)
     Beakers up. Partners,
     measure the volume and enter
     the data.
          (drones on)
     Gr'gan, record the data.
     Data sticks will be due
     today. Don't forget to
     leave yours with me before
     exiting the room.

LATER IN CLASS:

Bofsky is measuring a liquid into a
beaker. Gr'gan, a taller, mature fifteen-
year-old, hands Bofsky the necessary
supplies, recording the data on a hand-
held recording device.

Bofsky suddenly has trouble with the
assignment, and he looks up in panic.
Gr'gan speaks for the first time as he
hands a different beaker to Bofsky.

                    GR'GAN
          (very friendly)
     Look at that. I guess you
     really need this thing here.

Bofsky freezes, unable to go on, a frozen
expression on his face. Bofsky turns his
head away from Gr'gan.

                    BOFSKY
          (intensely, whispering)
     I've found one of them.

An intense look of purpose comes over
Bofsky's face as his expression shifts
from anger to a pleasant smile, and he

turns to Gr'gan. Gr'gan smiles back as
Bofsky takes the beaker.

INT. HALLWAY - DAY

A large double door is standing open.
BOFSKY is standing just outside as if
wanting to remain unseen. Rows of
fourteen- and fifteen-year-olds are seated
inside and muffled talking can be heard.

>   VOICE (Off Screen)
>   Being part of the
>   fourteen/fifteen dorms means
>   you should act *more* grown
>   up, not less. Your behavior
>   has been absolutely
>   unacceptable. Now, there
>   will be consequences.
>   Listen as I . . .

Bofsky grins widely as he heads off down
the hall.

INT. 14/15 DORM - DAY

Bofsky is prowling, checking out the names
on each bunk. As he walks up to one of
the many bunks, his finger points
purposefully at a tag that reads GR'GAN,
146c. Bofsky pulls the tag out and turns
it over to see more words. GR'GAN RHNST.

Bofsky smiles a very satisfied-looking
grin. He opens the locker beside the bunk
and rifles through the things there.
Opening a small container, he pulls out a
wad of money. He quickly stuffs it into a
pocket. He returns the rest of the items
to the locker and turns away.

Bofsky strides rapidly past the rest of the bunks, exiting the room.

INT - 'GLASS' DATA WORKSTATION - DAY

Bofsky and Gr'gan are seated at a shared 'glass' data console. It appears very old and abused. They are working on information that seems difficult, and a puzzled expression is frequently seen on Gr'gan's face.

> BOFSKY
> Hey, Gr'gan. You know, the test tomorrow and all, I could use some extra lab practice.
> (very friendly smile)
> I've got the key if you want to come with me.
> (holds it up)

> GR'GAN
> Sure. That would be great. I've never been really good at this, and if I don't get high marks this time, I might not get to go on. Together we seem to do all right. We make a good team, Willane. It'll sure be good to be able to get extra practice before the final scores are taken, the teacher offering you the lab after hours and all. See you after meals tonight.

Gr'gan grins, waves, and is off. Once he

is gone, Bofsky flips the filched key in
his hand.

> BOFSKY
> (to himself)
> Not exactly offering. Let's
> just say it's been made
> available.

Bofsky reaches a hand to his leg where he
begins to rub the seam of his pant leg.
The outline of a crudely sewn seam shows
where a small knife has been sewn into the
fabric.

FLASHBACK:

Bofsky, ten years old, pulls the knife out
of his pocket. As he holds it in his
hand, he suddenly clasps his fist around
it tightly.

BACK TO BOFSKY AT WORKSTATION:

Bofsky gives a laugh that doesn't sound
very pleasant at all.

INT. SCHOOL LAB - NIGHT

It is dark. Two sharp knocks disturb the
silence. The outline of a door appears as
someone opens it and leans in, and then
Gr'gan's voice breaks the silence.

> GR'GAN
> Hey, Willane. Are you here,
> yet? The lights are still
> out.

Gr'gan steps all the way in, the door

shutting behind him, letting total
darkness return. A sudden *OMPH* is heard,
as if Gr'gan has hit something.

>   GR'GAN (CONT'D)
>   (unafraid)
>   Hey! Willane, help!

Lights flood the room. Gr'gan is on the
floor. Gr'gan twists his upper body
around at the 'snick' sound of a small
knife opening. He suddenly starts moving
backwards along the floor.

Bofsky stands with a small collapsible
knife opened in his hand.

>   GR'GAN
>   Willane, what are you doing?
>   Why do you have that knife
>   out?

>   BOFSKY
>   Get off the pretend wagon,
>   Gr'gan. Your goons had my
>   eyes covered, but I could
>   still hear. You think I
>   didn't know you, couldn't
>   tell from your voice? I
>   haven't found the others,
>   but I bet you'll be glad to
>   tell me. At least you will
>   by the time I finish.

Bofsky twists the knife so it glints in
the overhead lights.

>   BOFSKY (CONT'D)
>   This little blade has been
>   by my side in more ways than

one for a very long time.
Tonight I finally get to put
it to use, payback for that
night you did all those
things to me.

            GR'GAN
     (sudden realization in his eyes)
Whoa, Willane. I didn't
know that was you. Honest.
Don't do this, Willane. We
had to do that. The
counselor told us we'd be
written up, kicked out if we
didn't. I never even saw
your face or knew who you
were. I know we said we
did, but we never did. I
promise.
     (pleading)
You gotta believe me,
Willane. We're friends, you
and me.

            BOFSKY
Friends! Liar! I could've
died. Unlucky for you I
didn't. Nobody came back to
help me. Nobody. You're
not my friend. I wanted a
friend, but you are a liar!

Bofsky raises his arm to cut Gr'gan; as
his coiled muscles tense to spring, he
feels something sudden and tight clamp his
wrist.

            TEACHER
So, that's where my lab key
went. An old-fashioned

security method to have even
at this ancient, worn-out
school, but easy to track.
This little altercation is
over.

With a flick of the man's hand, the knife
is taken from Bofsky.

INT.   COUNSELOR'S OFFICE - DAY

The desk is spotlessly clean except for a
data stick and an official looking
preprinted form. On the form in block
letters are the words FORCED INDUCTION,
MEGACORP MILITARY TRAINING ARM with a
blank line underneath. Just above the
paper is a data display on a rectangle of
glass suspended in the air. The same form
on the desk is also on the 'glass'
display. A hand brings up a stylus,
writing on the paper form. No writing
appears on the paper. Instead, the name
appears on the form displayed on the
'glass' display: WILLANE BARD BOFSKY.

As soon as the name appears on the
display, the same hand picks up the data
stick, pushing it into a slot beside the
glass. The computer-generated form seems
to suck down into the data stick. When
the word FINISHED appears on the glass,
the hand pulls out the stick.

The data stick is handed to another set of
hands, these with the sleeves of a black
uniform. As the man taking the data stick
walks away, on the other side of a glass
window, a boy sits on a chair with a
black-suited man standing on either side

of him. Each has a logo emblazoned across
his chest containing the letters M C. The
boy sitting on the chair is Bofsky.

ACT V - MY HOME IS SHIPSIDE

INT.   OPERATING THEATER - DAY (PRESENT)

BOFSKY stands in a crisp black military
outfit with the letters M C emblazoned
across the chest. This is an operating
room with a raised platform in the center
that has been used for an interrogation.
Bofsky is holding an instrument somewhat
like a baton. It is a NeuroShok stick.
Four other people are trying to look as
inconspicuous as possible. Two of these
people are HOLCUM and REZALTON. On the
table is what remains of a person. There
has been quite a bit of damage.

          BOFSKY
     Haul that mess out of here!
     Make sure it is gone before
     I return.

Bofsky slaps the NeuroShok stick down on
the table, spins on his heel, and exits,
slamming the door behind him. Holcum,
lets out a long-held breath. She is quite
beautiful although austere and no-
nonsense. She wears a similar uniform to
Bofsky's. Her uniform is less ornate,

indicating a marginally lower rank.

>   HOLCUM
> Je'Vark. Rezalton. Get
> those exhaust fans going.
> Thomps'n. Bag this and
> carry it to recycling.
> Stat! The gods know how
> soon Bofsky will have
> another one in need of this
> theater. Then the three of
> you grab a drum of
> Sterilspray and wash this
> down. Page me when
> complete. I'll be in my
> quarters.

>   REZALTON
>   (crisply, pointedly not looking at
>   the damage)
> Yes, Ser. Je'Vark, this
> way. Thomps'n, give us a
> minute, and we'll be back to
> help you out.

Holcum exits the chamber.

INT.   CORRIDOR - DAY (A FEW MINUTES LATER)

Holcum strides down a corridor with a full
glassine wall on the left side. Through
the wall is the blackness of space. No
stars are visible in the sky. Two distant
suns, one much larger than the other,
grace the sky. A beautiful planet is
floating in the blackness, one with
beautiful green landmasses, blue waters,
and a very yellow sky. Holcum does not
appear to notice.

                    HOLCUM
          (out loud, although to herself)
     Planets are all the same,
     places for groundies. Why
     would I want to look at a
     place I wouldn't even visit?
     My home is *shipside*.

Holcum walks down the corridor, slapping
at a panel on her right side, and the view
through the glassine wall suddenly
disappears as the glassine instantly turns
opaque.

ACT VI - DESPAIR ON SE'YAN'T

EXT.   SURFACE OF REJUVENANT/SE'YAN'T - DAY

ADHOR'K, beautiful and young in the
freshness of her re-birth, is on a verdant
ridge with the beauty of the planet
stretching behind her. The twin suns are
both low in the sky behind her, the ever-
present sea in the distance. She is
looking at the sky. Something is at her
feet. Her eyes close as the look of
sorrow on her face turns to one of anger.
She shakes her fist at the sky.

> ADHOR'K
> The dry-death is all you
> allowed her! Do you know
> what you've done? What
> you've taken? Do you care?

Adhor'k drops to her knees, her hands
gently stroking the mangled body before
her.

Adhor'k's tears fall on the dead woman
before her. The twin shadows cast by this
world's two suns suddenly lengthen, the
clouds behind Adhor'k moving rapidly

through the sky, the twin suns moving as
one toward the horizon, indicating several
hours have passed. The tears continue to
fall.

EXT. BEACH ON REJUVENANT/SE'YAN'T - DAY

The water is off to the right, the verdant
green of the inland to the left, and the
stones are just ahead. A very old RJORCK
is impatiently waiting. Adhor'k comes
into the scene from behind one of the
large stones. She drops a bag on the
washed rock beach and drops beside it.
She is seated, her knees high in front of
her, and she places her arms up and over
her head.

>   ADHOR'K
> I am sorry, Brother, Bringer
> of News. Violence has never
> been our way. We could not
> have known, not imagined.
> Must all die?

Adhor'k pauses as the whispering waters
sound in the distance; a gentle hand cups
her chin, forcing her face to look up,
exposing the streaks of tears.

>   ADHOR'K (CONT'D)
> An ocean of tears and she
> could not come back to me,
> Rjorck. At least *they* will
> not find her. She is safe
> in the high fields.

>   RJORCK
>   (kneeling, speaking with sudden
>   vigor)

I have a transport. Tell
all who will travel with me.
We will go offworld,
somewhere we can be safe,
hide. Until the humans
despair of finding that
which they cannot share. We
will share life. We will
return when our waters, our
lands are ours again. When
there is no more *death*
hanging over us in our lemon
sky. Do you know lemons,
Adhor'k? Not all from Earth
is wicked. Just this.
These madmen. They will
tire of our world
eventually. Tell all you
can find. We have little
time.

Rjorck tenderly brushes the tear streaks
from Adhor'k's face. He gazes longingly
at the waters of the seas. He turns again
to Adhor'k, pulling her to her feet,
urgency in his actions.

                    RJORCK
Remember, time is short.
Have all you can gather meet
me on the yellow plain south
of the Ribbon Waterfall. My
transport is hidden nearby.
Hurry!

Rjorck reaches beneath his tunic. He
withdraws a slab of nutrient bread and
places it in Adhor'k's hands.

                    RJORCK (CONT'D)
          This will give you strength
          for what is required of you.

                    ADHOR'K
          Not all are convinced, my
          brother. Not all have seen
          the many who have died the
          dry-death at the hands of
          the humans.

Adhor'k pulls her bag over her shoulder,
tearing off a chuck of the bread, and
dropping the rest in her bag. Her self-
control breaks.

                    ADHOR'K (CONT'D)
                 (with anguish)
          Ahhh! Rjorck! So many have
          died the dry-death! Is it
          even possible to go on?

                    RJORCK
                 (grasping her arms)
          Do you wish all to go to the
          dry-death? Many have. Many
          more will. *You* can help
          those who would be saved.
          You are a strong one who can
          do this! Take courage in
          your strength. Go, my
          sister!

Adhor'k turns and strides away.

Rjorck watches Adhor'k for a moment, and
his smile turns from encouragement,
leaving a face filled with sadness.

INT.   BRIDGE ON RJORCK'S TRANSPORT - DAY

Rjorck is inside his transport. He is at
the controls. He slams his hand down on
what must be an autopilot button. Things
on the console begin to light up as if the
ship is readying to get underway.

>   RJORCK
>   (urgently)
>   Leave everything! Come
>   aboard now!

EXT.   TRANSPORT AND REFUGEES - DAY

A group of dusty, bedraggled refugees are
approaching the transport. Some are
already boarding. Many are far behind.
Adhor'k looks up, sees the ship, and
rushes on board.

BACK TO RJORCK:

Rjorck turns to her. He reaches to touch
Adhor'k's arm.

>   RJORCK
>   Adhor'k, watch over this for
>   me. The transport is on
>   automatic, now. I must get
>   the others inside.

Rjorck turns to leave the control center.

BACK TO THE EXTERIOR OF THE TRANSPORT:

Rjorck runs down the ramp. He eyes the
autowarn lights by the door blinking from
green to yellow. As the lights blink from
yellow to a final red and the ramp begins

to swing closed, Rjorck lifts a final one
of his people to safety, and the landing
ramp folds into the belly of the ship.

The ship ascends. No flames are seen as
the propulsion systems move the ship
through the air. A tearing squeal is
heard off screen, and Rjorck twists to
view a different part of the sky.

Rjorck sees an incoming object leaving a
streak in the sky. It is the object
making the noise. The object's impact
with the transport shatters the transport
into flaming tendrils that fall from the
sky. Rjorck falls to his knees, his head
dropping to his chest.

Rjorck continues to collapse in anguish.
A small transport lands, and the hissing
release of its airtight seals is heard.
Rjorck remains bowed as the voices of
Bofsky and Holcum begin to speak.

>   BOFSKY
> Take that man! I know this
> one. From Earth. He will
> certainly have the
> information I require.
> Place him aboard my pod for
> transport to the ship.

>   HOLCUM
> Yes, CaptGen'l, Ser.

Holcum places a pair of ziptites around
Rjorck's wrists.

Bofsky turns to board the pod. He pauses
and looks back in Rjorck's direction.

                    BOFSKY
You will tell me what I
require, or your people's
secrets die with you. You
are the last.

Bofsky turns and strides up the ramp.

ACT VII – STOLEN CHILDHOOD

INT.   BOFSKY'S CHILDHOOD HOME – NIGHT (48 YEARS EARLIER)

The room is very dark with a small amount of light coming in from a bare window. A boy, obviously BOFSKY at about ten years old, stands by the bed. Two other people, a man and a woman, are sleeping side-by-side in the bed. The room is small, and the bedding is shabby. Bofsky reaches across the woman to take something from the man. When the man moves, Bofsky freezes. Eventually, the man begins to snore. Bofsky then slides what looks like a large wallet from inside the man's bedclothes. Bofsky turns to leave, then turns back to the bed. He bends as if to give the woman a kiss.

As Bofsky raises his head, a tear glistens on her cheek, left by Bofsky.

Bofsky reaches a hand to wipe his eyes. As he turns and walks away, the woman reaches up to her face as if to touch the tear.

EXT. ALONG A DUSTY ROAD - DAY

Bofsky is squatting in the dust beside a
dirt road. He is raggedly dressed and
very dirty. He is also barefoot. He
pulls the pouch from inside his shirt and
grins. Untying the pouch, Bofsky reaches
inside and pulls out paper money. He
stands and removes something from a
pocket.

Bofsky unfolds the item in his hand,
revealing a small folding knife. He opens
his palm, the knife resting inside. Then
he snaps his hand into a fist, the knife
still inside. He is grinning widely.

Bofsky stuffs the money into the pocket,
then returns the knife to the opposite
pocket. He wads the money pouch and
tosses it into a ditch, kicking a cloud of
dirt over it. He turns away and walks
away down the road.

LATER:

EXT. TOWN STREET - DAY

Bofsky is being bumped and pushed. Others
around him are a mix of very seedy-looking
people with others appearing more
comfortably prosperous. Bofsky is in a
town with open trading stalls down a
central street. There are doorways
visible leading to dark, unnamed rooms.
It seems Bofsky is being followed as he
furtively looks behind him. Occasionally,
one of the paper bills in his pocket slips
to the ground, and we see a rough
character stop to retrieve it.

A SHORT TIME LATER:

Bofsky is being bumped repeatedly as he
starts to cringe, an expression of fear on
his face. Finally, a set of arms grabs
and pulls Bofsky toward one of the dark
doorways.

Bofsky looks desperately at the passing
throng. A man glances at the boy.
Concern flashes on the man's face, then he
intentionally chooses to look away and
walk on.

INT. DARK ROOM - DAY

There is only one, small, dingy window.
The room is empty except for various
refuse strewn about. Bofsky is thrown
into a corner. THE MAN who has been
following Bofsky speaks to another man
beside him as he runs his hands over
Bofsky's body, under his clothing and
inside his pockets.

>   THE MAN
>   (with excitement)
>   Ahh! I told ya' it were
>   'ere. I saw 'im, out there,
>   'e was, money fallin' all
>   over th' ground, 'im yankin'
>   it up like no one'd notice.
>   I noticed, did I. And I
>   came for me share. There's
>   plenty for th' two of us.
>   (rough laughter)

The man empties Bofsky's pockets, tearing
away much of his clothing in the process.

Bofsky's eyes tear up, and he cringes each
time the man reaches out to touch him.

The man and his partner stuff the money in
a small bag, and they begin to walk
towards the door. The SECOND MAN stops
and grabs the first man's arm.

>   SECOND MAN
>   (intensely)
>   Do ya' tink 'e might rat?

>   THE MAN
>   (looks back, smiles)
>   Not when we get through wid
>   'im.

Both men step to Bofsky and begin kicking
him violently. Bofsky yells for them to
stop once or twice, then he just curls
into a ball, covering his face with his
arms.

After a time, Bofsky becomes limp. Blood
covers the floor.

>   THE MAN
>   That'll do. Dead boys tell
>   no tales.

>   SECOND MAN
>   (sharp laugh)
>   That's for sure.

EXT. SMALL COTTAGE/BOFSKY'S HOME - DAY

The small cottage is timeworn and weary.
The ground around the cottage is all dirt.
The sun is very bright, and the thump of
wooden wheels over a broken, hard surface

is heard off screen. With a screech, a
cart comes to a stop in front of the
cottage's roughly made door. Inside the
cart is Bofsky's severely beaten body.
The MAN from the earlier bedroom scene is
pulling the cart. He steps to the door.
He does not appear drunk, but he is rough,
disheveled, and obviously very hung-over.
He kicks the door open.

                    BIG MAN
        Woman! Come out here. I've
        brought you your thief. He
        couldn't even hang on to any
        of it. He let it be stolen
        no sooner than he reached
        town. Fool!

The big man releases the cart's tray,
letting Bofsky tumble to the ground, his
body landing half inside and half outside
the cottage. The WOMAN appears at the
door, instantly wailing at what she sees.

                    WOMAN
        Willy!
            (kneeling, looking up at the man)
        It's Willy, my poor little
        Willane. We have to do
        something. Please.

                    BIG MAN
            (growling)
        That's right, woman.
        Something has to be done.

The big man reaches beside the door to the
shovel hanging on the wall.

                    BIG MAN (CONT'D)
     Furthermore, I intend to do
     it.

The woman lets her tears fall on Bofsky's
face. She reaches for the hem of her
apron to use her tears to wipe away the
blood.

LATER:

The big man is standing alone. He is
erect, the shovel blade resting on the
hard ground, both his hands on the handle.
His eyes are closed, and he is breathing
hard and fast as if dealing with internal
issues. Expressions run across his face
as if an internal dialogue is tearing at
him. He begins to pace, and finally
stops, apparently reaching some sort of
answer to his dilemma. His features
smooth, almost become pleasant.

The big man walks up to the woman, still
bent over the boy. She glances up at his
approach. The big man reaches down almost
tenderly to touch the woman's shoulder.

The woman's face turns from sorrow to
anger as her eyes lock on the shovel.

                    WOMAN
     No!
          (flinging the big man's hand away)
     You'll not beat him again,
     you always so angry, so
     drunk because you couldn't
     take his father's place.
     He's my *son*. You've beaten
     me, and I've taken it.

You've raped me, and I've
lain under your stink the
while, you grunting on top
of me, making me ill.

We see the woman gently place the boy's
head on her wadded apron and stand.

She lashes out with her hand, leaving red
streaks across the big man's face.

A surprised look comes across the big
man's face, the red streaks clear and
brightening.

> WOMAN
> I'll kill you first before I
> let you beat him again. You
> think I don't know what you
> intend, that shovel in your
> hand? Look at him. Look!
> Look what you've done. It's
> no thanks to you he's not
> dead on the ground, you
> beating him again all for a
> few credits. I should have
> kicked you out of my house
> the first time you touched
> him. Don't come near us
> again.
> (shakes her fist at him)

The big man steps forward, confusion on
his face. As he does so, the woman
explodes at him in a leap, knocking the
man down.

The woman's fists hit the big man as she
sits on top of him. The big man twists,
fighting for air. The shovel is still in

his hand, and he swings it, hitting the woman again and again. Finally, all is still, and the big man lies under the woman, panting. Blood is dripping on the man's face as his hand drops the shovel, now stained with blood. The big man rubs his hand on his face, and he looks at his fingers. A dawning realization of what he's done shows in the expression of dismay on his face.

The big man sobs. The boy moves slightly, making a scraping sound. The big man turns to look the boy's way with hope for understanding on his face. The big man gently lays the woman's body aside and goes to the boy. He kneels at the boy's side.

One of the boy's eyes opens. The expression on the boy's face hardens as we see the eye close.

The big man closes his eyes, and his face tightens in despair and resignation. He stands, steps over the boy, and walks into the cottage.

INT.   INSIDE OF COTTAGE - DAY

The big man is slouched in his chair, and there are empty containers of drink at his side, some turned over with fluid spilled. His eyes are opened wide and staring. Small flying insects land on them. The man does not flinch.

BACK TO BOY:

The boy is lying in the doorway, and his

mother's dead body lies near him. He is
still breathing, and his eyes are closed.
Shadows of clouds flicker across the boy's
face, the shadows lengthen, and finally
darkness arrives.

ACT VIII - THE PAST IS NOW

EXT.   MEGACORP MILITARY PARADE GROUNDS - DAY

A row of incredibly tall flagpoles surrounds a wide-open parade ground. Surrounding this parade ground is a series of two- and three-story buildings and colonnaded walkways. The far side is almost difficult to make out. The flags snap in the breeze above rows of suited cadets, career military persons, and battle-scarred veterans, crisp and erect in their dress blacks, facing severely ahead. Atop a slender tower surveying the parade grounds, small and barely visible, a VOICE rings out from unseen speakers.

> VOICE
> For the protection of all
> peoples living in systems
> both near and far, those
> living on industrial as well
> as pastoral worlds,
> occupants of minor worlds
> and asteroids, thank you for
> your attendance today.

Those viewing the parade grounds in person
move as if standing a little prouder at
the words they are hearing.

Bands of various types and dress swell the
air with volume, fading in intensity only
as the triumphant voice continues.

                    VOICE (CONT'D)
          For many years, humanity has
          suffered needlessly.
          Certain groups of people
          have hoarded the bounty of
          their world rather than
          sharing for the greater
          good. That time is
          finished. Let our peoples
          raise a shout of triumph, a
          cry of victory. The mighty
          arm of our military division
          has returned to us
          victorious, the rabble on
          our mining world vanquished.
          An unlimited resource our
          corporation has bargained
          and paid dearly for, the
          resources for this
          corporation, for *Earth* to
          triumph in its supremacy
          over all other worlds, has
          been regained. Raise a
          shout to our men and women
          who stand before you, the
          vanquishers of the rabble,
          the supreme force of might,
          our right arm, literally,
          the MegaCorp Military Arm.
               (roar of approval from the crowd)
          But wait.
               (pause)

> Here in person is the one
> who single-handedly led our
> troops in their successful
> attack, the career officer
> who selflessly stepped into
> danger to ensure the
> continued economic success
> of our great corporation's
> endeavors, our very own
> OverSergeant Ma'jene Holcum!

Holcum is sitting on the platform with the speaker and a number of other military personnel. Her face momentarily tightens at the mention of her name.

Flashback:

EXT. BATTLE-SCARRED WORLD - DAY

A devastated planet stretches into the distance. This is a war zone, and by the extent of the damage, apparently has been for many years. The light is filled with airborne debris, and the glowing tips of numerous weapons move in the haze as the sporadic rat-a-tat or *zzst* of small weapons fire is heard.

Holcum is in black, crouched on the crumbling pavement. Black-suited troops back her up. The troops' suits flicker into invisibility as they step and move about the debris. Holcum's head pivots left and right as if sensing something no one else can.

FLASHBACK TO AN EVEN EARLIER MEMORY:

INT. HOLCUM'S CHILDHOOD HOME - DAY

This is Holcum's war damaged childhood home. Images have a sepia-toned look, unevenly colored as if intentionally forgotten and only remembered by accident. The frames are out of square, the action jerky, as if remembered in the disjointed and haphazard way a child would store away such events. The distinctive section of wall the girl, Holcum, was hiding behind as a child is prominently seen. The view is what Holcum's childhood eyes would have seen.

MONTAGE:

An arm of one of her parents is in view.

Smoke fills the sky above the roofless dwelling.

Black-suited soldiers search through the debris of the home.

BACK TO BATTLE SCENE:

Holcum glances to her right. She sees the distinctive section of the wall she had hidden behind as a child. Holcum lets out a blood-curdling scream.

Holcum charges directly ahead as a primitive explosive shell takes out the three soldiers just to her right. She runs through the familiar remains of her childhood home, massacring the remains of the resistance movement before her team even has a chance to act.

SIX MONTHS LATER:

Holcum is reading a note she has just
pulled up on her 'glass' data unit. The
cubicle's door is not quite shut, and an
undercadet is nervously poised as if to
escape as soon as given permission.

> HOLCUM
> Teat-sucking cowards! They
> want *what*? They think I
> *want* this? That I *want* the
> *dirt* of another mother-
> scrubbing world on my boots?
> Can't they ever just *promote*
> without forcing us to *dance*
> for it?

Holcum grabs a data stick and yanks it
from her 'glass' data unit. Finally, she
notices the cadet.

> HOLCUM (CONT'D)
> And you're still here?
> Gods, get out of my sight!

He slips out just as a handy boot slams
into the wall where he has been standing.

The opening line of HOLCUM's orders is
just visible on the 'glass' data terminal.

CONGRATULATIONS. PROCEED WITH ALL HASTE
TO EARTH FOR YOUR UPCOMING PROMOTIONAL
CEREMONY . . ..

BACK TO HOLCUM ON THE PLATFORM:

Holcum stands erect in the breeze. Hands

pin her new insignia onto her lapels.
Those around Holcum snap to attention as
Holcum is saluted.

>   VOICE
> Congratulations, Corp'lMaj'r
> Ma'jene Holcum. You deserve
> this.

INT. TRANSPORT - DAY

Holcum is still in her full-dress uniform
dropping into a seat on a transport back
into space. A new BraveHeart medal is
entwined through the epaulets on her
shoulder. She reaches with a cloth and
wipes the dust from her shoes, her disgust
evident on her face.

>   HOLCUM
> Great gods from the ancient
> past, I hope I never have to
> set foot on another planet.
> Moles. Nothing but slugs.
> Ground crawlers. That's all
> planets are good for.

Holcum glances through the transport's
viewing wall at a ship hanging overhead in
the blackness of space.

>   HOLCUM (CONT'D)
> My home is up *there*.
> Shipside.

Holcum tosses the dirt-stained cloth in
the disposal chute, and she leans back and
closes her eyes.

INT. BOFSKY AND HIS FRIENDS - NIGHT

The lighting is secretive and dim. All
that can really be seen are the faces of
four seventeen-year-olds: BOFSKY, RENHANT,
JER'SON, and BARN'T.

> BOFSKY
> How long have we been on
> this ship, here in the
> academy? The training
> commanders never let any of
> the cadets go planetside.
> Barn't, Jer'son, even you,
> Renhant. You've been here
> the longest, too. We're all
> uppercadets, every one of
> us. None of us have gone
> planetside, not even once.
> We can do this, men.
>   (bores his stare into the others)
> Men, what'll it be? Spend
> the next four months doing
> the dirty by ourselves in
> extra-long showers, or a
> wild excursion with a wild
> woman, turning us into men
> the way it is supposed to
> happen?

> RENHANT
>   (pleading)
> They can strip us of our
> academy credits and send us
> to grunt the front line for
> something like this, Bofsky.
> You know that. Shrinking
> varneys, we all do. Yeah, I
> admit, my hand's way too

familiar with my 'pent-up
manhood,' as you like to
say. But varneys, Bofsky, a
good shake-down each time we
shower, and we can make it
through. This is *crazy*.
Just a few months for most
of us, eleven for you,
Barn't, and we have officer
status. Planetside is our
due, then.

Renhant pauses. He looks around at the
excited looks on the faces of his friends
and drops his head, giving in.

INT. SHUTTLE - DAY

The four boys from the previous scene are
seated on the shuttle wearing officer
uniforms. Through the glassine wall,
their academy training ship recedes from
view.

            RENHANT
     (whispering, leaning over to Bofsky)
     How did you get that pass?
     There's no way you can dup
     them. They're foolproof.
     Give, Bofsky.

            BOFSKY
     Here.
     (hands the pass to Renhant)
     Run your fingernail down the
     centerline. Tell me what
     you feel.

            RENHANT
     Hey.

>   (grins)
>   A seam. Two cards put
>   together?

>   BOFSKY
>   All too easy.
>   (slips it down inside his officer
>   overjacket)
>   My only challenge was
>   getting my hands on an
>   adhesive that wouldn't give
>   way while it was being
>   inspected and our escapade
>   approved. Thanks, Jer'son.
>   (slaps his friend's back)
>   You are a lifesaver. Or,
>   more accurately put, a
>   manhood saver. I admit
>   that's even better.
>   (laughs out loud)

EXT. STREET SCENE ON THE SURFACE OF THE
PLANET - NIGHT

A park is to the right. Benches are along
the street facing the sidewalk. There are
periodic streetlights. The whorehouse is
across the street. There is an office
where customers pay, then stairs and a row
of doors, and some are open and some
closed, indicating whether the prostitute
is occupied or not. Bofsky is speaking
through a sliding window, and the other
three boys are standing behind him.

>   BOFSKY
>   (incredulous)
>   How many credits?

Bofsky makes a face and turns to his

fellow uppercadets.

                    BOFSKY (CONT'D)
          We've a problem, men.
          Between the four of us,
          there's not enough credits
          to get even two girls. We
          need to get together and
          make a plan.

                    JER'SON
               (disgusted)
          Plan? Are you going to
          steal the credits, Bofsky?
          Or do they just come out of
          the sky? Better, let's all
          reach into the depths of our
          magic pockets and bring a
          magic credit stick - oops!
          That's not a credit stick!
          That's my ready, willing,
          and very frustrated shake-
          down shower buddy. Great
          plinkerpups, all that work,
          these officer overjackets,
          the time we spent planning
          is all for nothing.
          Tomorrow night I'll still be
          doing hand rhythm exercises.
          One, two, three, four.
          Stand up; give me more.
          Bofsky!

                    BOFSKY
          No, no. Wait.

Bofsky motions them over to a bench on the
street.

                    BOFSKY (CONT'D)
Look at this, men. See
those doors, all those guys
going in and out? We only
need one girl. I'll pool
our credits and go back.

                  ALL THREE BOYS
Whoa.
     (all three take a step back)
Why you?

                      BOFSKY
You don't understand. Once
I get the room, I'll let you
guys come in, too. What'll
she know? Just that I like
it four times.

                      BARN'T
Bofsky. Try eight times.
I'm going for at least two,
myself.
     (laughter from the others)

All the boys start pulling out their
money.

LATER:

Three of the teenagers are sitting on the
bench, watching the door, sated looks of
satisfaction settled on their rumpled
features. They laugh as Renhant stumbles
through the door, his overjacket under his
arm, shoes in his hand, fastening his
pants as he runs to them, frantic.

                      BARN'T
Afraid you'll get caught?

Or were you unable to, eh-
hem, perform satisfactorily,
Renhant? Own up, now.
　　(laughs)

　　　　　RENHANT
Hey, you. There's a
problem. A big problem.

　　　　　BARN'T
Don't josh around with us,
Renhant. What do you mean,
problem?

　　　　　RENHANT
Well, I went in, catching
the door just as you were
leaving, Jer'son. You
looked at me, jerking your
head to show me to go on in.
Well, I did. Just like you
said, Jer'son. There she
was, waiting, still-like. I
thought she was ready for
me, so I got my clothes off
quick as I could. Man, was
I ready. So ready. Like
never before.

　　　　　JER'SON
　　(grins)
Enough of that, Renhant.
Paint us a picture we want
to have in our heads, and
you're not it, trust me.

　　　　　RENHANT
Well, there I was, ready,
and I climbed on the
platform. You know how it

was pretty dark. Well, I
did it, you know. And she
never moved the whole time.
Not once. Not a sound,
either. After, I got off
and began to wonder. I felt
her chest, and by all the
ancients, I think she was
dead.

                  JER'SON
C'mon, Renhant. If you felt
her chest and didn't go
again, *you're* dead.
     (laughs)

                  RENHANT
Guys, I propped the door
open. I just did it with a
dead person. Go see. We
killed her.

His face grows paler as he talks, his body
suddenly shivering.

            RENHANT (CONT'D)
She's dead. Maybe *I* killed
her.

                  BOFSKY
     (to JER'SON)
He's spooked. Go run over
and see. Come right back.

Bofsky turns back to Renhant, gently
slapping his face.

            BOFSKY (CONT'D)
It's okay, Renhant.
Jer'son's going to check.

Don't sweat it.

INT. SHUTTLE - NIGHT

The four panicked boys are sitting in the
dark on a shuttle, watching the falling
planet through the clearwall beside their
seats. None are speaking. There is
desperation in the set of their eyes
telling of what they know.

FLASHBACK:

Below, on the planet, in a lonely room, a
dead woman lies, and the evidence of the
boys' time spent with her is strewn across
her bed, the signs telling of four boys'
spent manhood waiting in her patient
embrace.

BACK TO SHUTTLE:

On one boy's face is an expression of
anger. Another's face is blank. Yet
another boy has tears leaking from his
eyes. The shuttle is empty except for the
four friends.

INT. OFFICE ON THE PLANET'S SURFACE - DAY

A port OFFICER is sitting at his desk. He
is spinning a stylus on its surface. On
his 'glass' in front of him is information
about the death of the prostitute. This
information is in a box at the top of the
glass with additional information
scrolling quickly across the bottom of the
glass. Suddenly, he taps his stylus, and
the scrolling stops. He reaches to the
glass and backs up the information a

couple of strokes.

A look of understanding appears on his
face as he hits his forehead with his
palm. He taps a comm button on his desk.

>   OFFICER
> Duty-Assistant Rovek? That
> trainer, the *Ev'ntu'l-
> Landfall,* can you get the
> downship log of officers
> who've been planetside this
> maneuver? I need DNA
> matches for all of them. We
> can't hold the ship, so that
> only gives us until tonight.
> I believe departure is set
> for 23:00 L.A.T. Do this
> stat. Can do?

His hand releases the comm button, and he
returns to his data access unit, barely
acknowledging the response that snaps from
the comm.

With the stylus, the officer reaches out
and repeatedly taps the words
Ev'ntu'lLandfall on the glass of the data
access unit.

INT. BOFSKY'S DARK QUARTERS - DAY

The lights are dim, and a door opens.

>   JER'SON
> Bofsky? Are you there?
>   (no answer)
> Bofsky?

                    BOFSKY
          (mumbles, barely heard)
Yeah, Jer'son? What's so
important? My brain's kinda
busy now and all.

                    JER'SON
You haven't heard, then.
Ship's pulling downship
lists, looking for officers
who spent time planetside.
Us. Willane, they're
looking for *us.* Ship got a
requisition for DNA records
over the ship-link before
the feed went down. We're
running all officer DNA
records and shipping the
info down planetside, stat.
Willane, they're looking for
us.

                    BOFSKY
          (sits up)
We're not on the officer's
list. None of us. If they
send the profiles of the
officers, they won't get a
match. It's only a few
units 'til departure. That
gives us a little time.

                    JER'SON
But, Willane. Remember that
adhesive? When I got it, I
had to let someone know what
it was for. Zen'ri, in the
stores. He knows it was for
a pass. What if he puts it
all together? We've got to

                    106

make sure.

Jer'son looks toward the door repeatedly,
running his hand through his hair, his
nervousness apparent.

>   JER'SON (CONT'D)
>   Renhart and Barn't are
>   getting him to meet them in
>   the utility corridor,
>   feeding him a line. He'll
>   go. He'll be scared not to.
>   Dog-sheesh, I'm scared.
>   Let's go, Willane, and make
>   sure the ship's gone before
>   Zen'ri can rat.
>   (heads to utility corridor)

INT. UTILITY CORRIDOR - DAY

The four friends are standing around, plus
a new boy is with them, ZEN'RI. Zen'ri is
animated, looking from face to face, his
eyes flicking around the interior of the
utility corridor.

>   ZEN'RI
>   You four. Hey, you
>   shouldn't even have a key
>   code to this corridor.

Realization dawns on Zen'ri's face, and he
draws a deep breath, his skin flushing.

>   ZEN'RI (CONT'D)
>   *You*. That's what all the
>   flurry has been about.
>   There *were* no officers
>   offship that period. That's
>   why records keep coming up

incomplete. They *are*
incomplete. That adhesive
you wanted.
   (turns to look at Jer'son)
You said it was for a
damaged pass. You forged a
pass. That is supposed to
be impossible. They're
foolproof. But you found a
way. You must have glued
half of an expired pass with
half of a good one. You did
that down there on the
planet, what they are
looking for DNA about. I
have to go and let them
know.
   (edges toward door)

        BOFSKY
We can't let you do that,
Zen'ri. I'm sorry. What
would it look like for four
academy uppercadets, just
months from graduation, to
be implicated in some
unsavory planetside
politics? Just look at it
from MegaCorp's viewpoint.
That's what they'd think.
Now, once the ship is
underway, everything will be
okay. You'll go back to
ship's stores, and we'll
graduate, promoted to a
battlecruiser. We'll never
meet again, and life will be
fine and dandy.

Bofsky pushes himself closer to the scared

cadet.

Zen'ri makes a sudden dash for the door.
In a heart-stopping frenzy of motion, his
four subjugators leap after him. Arms
scramble and legs fly. All four friends
show injuries of some sort or another, but
Zen'ri cannot tell. His head rests
against the corner of a metal flange, his
eyes twitching open and slowly closing,
his body's muscles dancing in an erratic
jerk.

As the four teenagers watch, a pool of red
begins to seep from beneath Zen'ri's head.
They turn to look at one another. They
suddenly bolt, this time with no one to
stop them. Zen'ri's muscles continue to
run their tired dance until his eyes stay
open for good, his life-blood finally
exhausted on the utility corridor floor.

ACT IX - RJORCK GOES HOME

INT. RJORCK'S PRIVATE STUDY ON EARTH -
DAY

RJORCK is sitting in front of a fire
crackling in a fireplace. He is ancient
beyond ancient. The light from the flames
flickers over his mottled skin. He
presses his hands on the arms of the
chair, its leather shifting as his old
man's weight overcomes the leather's
groans. Unsteadily, he pushes himself to
a standing position, pausing to regain
long-forgotten balance. What appears to
be a NURSE walks quickly in, flustered
that Rjorck has not called him.

      NURSE
Here. Let me help you to
the car. I'll get your man
to begin to shut the house
down.

      RJORCK
  (gravelly and thick)
Thank you, Shn'dri. Thank you.

The nurse helps Rjorck shuffle to the

door, exiting the dwelling.

INT.   SPACESHIP - DAY

A ship's corridor stretches out lined by
glassed-in bunks. However, this is a much
newer model with more bunks and a changed
configuration. The opening process of the
interstellar flight bunks is the same.
Similar events repeat themselves as a
crewman walks through slapping the red
panels at each bunk. The doors and lights
work much more evenly. The same cold fog
spills into the corridor. From off screen
comes the rough coughing of a very old
man.

INT.   BUNK - DAY

Rjorck rests inside the bunk, his eyes
closed. He is very old, and his face is
very lined. He barely breathes, and his
face flinches repeatedly as if in great
pain. The familiar pack is placed on his
chest, but this time someone reaches in to
help place it to Rjorck's lips. Rjorck
continues to cough.

EXT.   SPACESHIP - DAY

Rjorck is being carried from the ship on a
stretcher. He reaches a parchment-skinned
hand to brush one of those carrying him,
BERIAN.

                    RJORCK
     Who?

                    BERIAN
     Berian, and Wolmn, too.

Adhor'k will be with you
soon. Rest, beloved. Rest.

Rjorck relaxes his hand. He closes his
eyes and seems to sleep.

EXT. STONE - DAY

A stone is being washed by the sea. The
water rushes up over the stone, then
retreats. This happens over and over as a
whispered VOICE OVER in many layers of
voices fades in and out.

          WATERS (VOICE OVER)
It is your time, friend
Rjorck. We await you. Our
embrace is yours. Come to
us. Do not make us wait.
Renewal will be yours.

EXT. RJORCK - DAY

The hand of a young woman, ADHOR'K,
strokes Rjorck's brow, running down his
cheek and chin.

          ADHOR'K
    (whispered)
Rjorck, I remember the
time . . .

The sounds of the water on the stones are
soon heard over Adhor'k's whisper.

ACT X - JO'N AND THE MARBLE

EXT. REZALTON'S CHILDHOOD HOME - DAY

Rom'n Rezalton, thirteen, is just into the
first burst of adolescence, not yet with
the true makings of manhood on his body,
but clearly no longer a small boy. He is
tall but appears younger than when we
first saw him earlier, perhaps due in part
to the fit of his clothing or the
insecurity of his actions. He is slender
with clean, even features. His skin and
hair are very pale. He is wearing a
fresh, sharply creased uniform. By his
side is a crisp new duffel sitting in the
dirt. Standing around him we see a
mother, a father, and several younger
sisters. The rest of Rezalton's family
are dark-haired with golden skin. All are
clean but very poorly dressed. None look
well fed. All smile, making them appear
very proud of him. The boy's hand
absentmindedly reaches to caress a pocket
on his duffel.

FLASHBACK:

INT. BED ALCOVE - DAY

113

Rezalton pulls items from a rough wooden beam, obviously a ceiling rafter above a cramped bed. He holds each item in his hand for a long moment before going on to the next. He displays a horse carved on the surface of a nutshell and a glass eye/marble.

He packs the items carefully in the duffel on his bed.

BACK TO REZALTON OUTSIDE HIS FAMILY'S COTTAGE:

Rezalton takes his hand off the duffle. His eyes redden and fill with tears.

FLASHBACK:

An envelope is handed to Rezalton's parents. Rezalton's mother withdraws a piece of paper from inside and holds it in a quavering hand. The mother collapses with a wail; the letter is let go, fluttering to the ground.

MONTAGE:

A progression of memories is experienced.

A shipping box is being stuffed in a chest, unopened.

Rezalton, about nine, pulls the shipping box out, going through what is obviously someone's last possessions. He holds different items to his face, taking deep breaths, and then closing his eyes before picking up another item.

A quick series of these flash by: an older
brother, dark like the parents, playing a
game with a ball in the woods, laughing
and running; the same brother, shaving and
wiping his face with a small towel, a grin
on his face; the same brother's hand
digging in freshly tilled soil; the
brother crawling into bed with Rezalton,
the brother's hair still wet from bathing,
snuggling with Rezalton against the
obvious cold.

Rezalton pulls a brand-new shirt from the
box. Tearing the plastic wrap away, he
pulls it on, the sleeves much too long.

Rezalton is again wearing the shirt, this
time fitting better, but very worn.

BACK TO REZALTON OUTSIDE HIS FAMILY'S
COTTAGE:

The mother's hand starts to caress
Rezalton's cheek as a tear rolls out of a
reddened eye. Rezalton breaks from her
touch and runs for the waiting transport.

INT. WAITING TRANSPORT - DAY

Rezalton is leaning the side of his face
against the glassine that allows him to
see outside the transport. His breath
keeps fogging up a small area. Outside,
his parents and sisters are waving, the
mother wiping her eyes, the father
standing off to the side under a tree.
More tears roll down Rezalton's face. His
hand reaches to his duffel, and he fingers
the items he has stored safely inside.

EXT. CITY SCENE - NIGHT (FIVE YEARS
EARLIER)

The city street sparkles as if it has
rained recently. Lighted, glassed-in
shops display goods of all kinds. JO'N
and Rezalton are heard off screen before
they are actually visible. Streetlights
dot the sidewalk with pedestrian benches
spaced periodically. Shop signs are very
discretely placed within the windows
themselves. Jo'n, a man about nineteen,
and Rezalton, a boy of eight, walk down
the street. Rezalton has his arm around
the man's waist, and the man's arm is
around Rezalton's shoulder.

> JO'N
> You should have seen 'em,
> Rom'n. Fair-haired beauties
> as far as my eyes could see.
> All just waiting for me to
> walk up and give 'em a kiss.

Rezalton looks up into Jo'n's face. Jo'n
has an amused smile. He looks down at
Rezalton, then looks up, perusing the shop
windows as if moving on to other matters
in his mind. Rezalton continues to look
up expectantly as the pair continue to
walk down the street.

> REZALTON
> Did you?
>   (long pause)
> Well, did you?

> JO'N
>   (glancing down, one eyebrow cocked)

116

Did I what, little bro?

Jo'n looks away as if shopping in the window displays. Rezalton grins and punches Jo'n in the stomach with a fist.

> REZALTON
> You know what! Did you kiss
> 'em?

Rezalton wraps both arms around Jo'n's waist, burying his face in Jo'n's stomach. Jo'n runs his hands all over Rezalton's body, tickling him. Rezalton finally erupts into laughter.

> JO'N
> Kiss 'em? You want to know
> if I kissed 'em? I'll tell
> you what I did. I went up
> to one girl . . .

Jo'n picks up Rezalton, one arm under the boy's legs, the other behind his back, holding him to his face, twirling him around, and blowing on his stomach as Rezalton howls with laughter.

> JO'N
> I went up to one girl, and I
> grabbed her just like I've
> got you.

Jo'n holds Rezalton in the air, the boy holding on to Jo'n's arms as he stops twirling.

> REZALTON
> Then what, Jo'n? Then what?
> Tell me!

> (pauses, pants with excitement)
What did you do then, Jo'n?
Kiss her?

          JO'N
Nah. I didn't kiss her.
Nothing like that. I asked
her to marry me! And do you
know what she did?

          REZALTON
     (big grin)
No, Jo'n. What did she do?

Jo'n drops Rezalton in a quick motion,
easily catching him, with Rezalton's face
nose-to-nose with Jo'n's. Both Jo'n's
arms are wrapped tightly around Rezalton.
A huge smile is on Jo'n's face.

As he speaks, along with the brilliance of
his smile, tears threaten to erupt from
Jo'n's eyes.

          JO'N
She kissed ME! Just like
this!

Jo'n plants raspberry kisses repeatedly
all over Rezalton's face as Rezalton tries
to pull away, howling with laughter at the
unexpected ending to the story.

LATER:

It is the same evening in the city. A
streetlight stands over a park bench just
back from the curb. An occasional person
moves in front of the still-lighted store
windows in the background.

It is obviously later than before as
several of the stores are clearly closed.
Off to the left a food establishment has
an open storefront. Several people are in
line at the counter. One is given what
looks like a pizza-shaped package and
walks away with it. The package is not
boxed. Instead, the clerk has deftly and
effortlessly wrapped it with a type of
butcher paper as if this is a practiced
and repeated event.

On the park bench, Jo'n is lighted by the
streetlight. He is leaning back, one leg
crossed. His left arm is resting on the
back of the bench, his hand in a loose
fist. In the other, Jo'n is holding what
appears to be a slice of pizza as he takes
a bite, pulling the slice away from his
mouth, catching the stringy topping as he
does so.

Jo'n glances down to see Rezalton turning
something over in his hand. Rezalton is
looking intently at it. Next to Rezalton
is the wadded paper remains of his own
meal.

Jo'n takes notice of what Rezalton is
looking at and sits up.

> JO'N
What's that, little bro?

Jo'n reaches down to put his slice of
pizza on the wadded paper on the park
bench.

                    JO'N (CONT'D)
          Let me see that.

                    REZALTON
               (holding up the object)
          It was there just by the
          curb. I saw the streetlight
          shine in it. I don't know
          what it is.

Jo'n takes the object and holds it up to
the light from the streetlight.

                    JO'N
          Hmm. Shine *in* it? I've
          heard about this before. It
          can only mean one thing. I
          think you've found the Magic
          All-Seeing Eye.

Jo'n looks at his brother, pauses, and
then waves the object in front of the
streetlight over their heads. It is a
large glass marble with something inside
that looks like flames when it catches the
light. Jo'n cuts his eyes to Rezalton,
sees he has his attention, and lets a grin
flash across his lips. He quickly stifles
it.

                    JO'N
          Many years ago there were
          these two brothers. But
          they were like one. Two
          bodies, one soul. One mind.

As Jo'n holds the object up, there is an
obvious glow in the marble. It seems to
be a flickering flame. We see Rezalton's
eyes remain glued on the marble as Jo'n

                       120

continues.

INTERCUT SCENES AS STORY PROGRESSES:

The events of Jo'n's story are seen in
live action, including two brothers and a
horned apparition (the magic man).
Occasionally, the images of Jo'n and
Rezalton appear as the story continues.
As the continuous voiceover from Jo'n and
Rezalton weave the events together, the
muted sound from the events in Jo'n's
story continue to be heard. The magic man
is a horned apparition at times, and when
he is not wearing his headdress, simply an
old man at the end of a too long life.

                    JO'N
          One heart. What one brother
          thought, the other knew.
          What one brother loved, the
          other adored. No matter how
          far they traveled apart,
          they were always together.
          One heart. One mind,
          remember? Don't forget
          that. It's important.

                    REZALTON
          Why is it important, Jo'n?
          Is that all the story?

                    JO'N
          I'm going to tell you why it
          is so important. And it is
          very important. So you must
          remember it always. One
          heart. One mind. No matter
          how far they traveled, they
          were always together. One

day a great magic man knew
something the brothers
didn't. He knew a great war
was coming. The brothers
would be separated for a
very long time. This great
magic man knew how much they
meant to each other. He
knew these brothers were
one, even though they lived
in different bodies. So the
magic man decided to help
the brothers.

REZALTON
How did he do that, Jo'n?
Did he make the war go away?

JO'N
No, Rom'n. He did something
much more difficult. Over
many years he had gathered
one grain of sand from each
of a thousand worlds, all
the worlds where the war was
going to happen, every world
where the one brother would
have to go to fight this
war, and the magic man cast
a spell. Now, this was no
easy spell. This was a
spell that took many days
and many nights. The magic
man couldn't sleep or eat
until this spell was
finished, and he was very
tired and hungry by the time
the spell was complete. In
fact, he was so tired and
hungry, he couldn't even

take the magic he'd created
and share it with the
brothers.

                REZALTON
Did he die? I hope he
didn't die, Jo'n.

                JO'N
He didn't die, not then,
Rom'n. The brothers, the
ones who were the same
person, they knew the magic
man was tired and hungry.

                REZALTON
How did they know? Did
someone tell them?

                JO'N
        (laughing out loud)
Sometimes people just know
things. The brothers knew
and went to see the magic
man, taking him food and a
blanket. When they got
there, the magic man was
very weak, too weak to eat.
The brothers were too late.
The magic man was going to
die. But before he did, he
told the brothers the magic
he had made for them.

                REZALTON
What magic? Like a magic
credit stick? With lots of
credits on it?

                    JO'N
              (laughing again)
No, better. The magic man
used up all his magic making
what he made. That's why he
was so weak. It wasn't the
food or sleep. He didn't
need food or sleep to live.
Oh, he liked to eat and
sleep, but he needed his
magic more. And he had used
it up in making this special
ball.

Jo'n holds the marble up, looking intently
into its center, as if he can see
something far away.

                    JO'N (CONT'D)
Many years before, the magic
man had taken all the sands
from the thousand worlds and
used his magic to change it
into many Magic Glass Eyes.
Over the many years of
helping others with his
Magic Eyes, he had used them
up. Now, he had made this
one his most powerful Magic
Eye. The very one I'm
holding right here in my
hand. The magic man held it
out to the two brothers. In
a voice that was very weak,
so weak the two brothers
that were one person had to
lean in very close, he spoke
to the two brothers who were
really one person.
              (softer, directly to Rezalton)

The magic man had put all his mighty magic into this last Magic Eye, he told the brothers. No matter how far apart they were, the Magic Eye would help them be together. As long as one brother kept the eye with him, the other brother could look through the eye and see the first brother. Then a glow passed from the magic man's fingertips to the Magic Eye, the last of his magic, and he died.

REZALTON

He died? How's that a good ending?

JO'N

It's not the ending, little bro. The brothers carried this Magic Eye for many years. The one brother did go off to war. He left the magic eye behind, and anytime the war became hard, or the brother saw too many bad things in the war, he could just close his eyes and see his brother through the Magic Eye. And that made the war not so bad. Then when he came home from the war, the brothers were one again, and the magic man spoke to them one more time.

                    REZALTON
Jo'n! The magic man can't
speak. He's dead!

                    JO'N
Yes, Rom'n, the magic man is
dead. But remember, all his
magic went into the Magic
Eye. It was his magic that
spoke.

                    REZALTON
What did it say?

                    JO'N
It told the brothers, now
that they were together
again, they didn't need the
Magic Eye anymore. It told
them there were other
brothers that were the same
person, just in two
different bodies, just like
we are, isn't that right,
Rom'n?

                    REZALTON
That's right, Jo'n. I'm
you, and you're me.

Rezalton leans even closer to Jo'n, as if
he can actually make the two of them into
one person. Jo'n holds the marble out to
Rezalton.

                    JO'N
The magic told the brothers
to put the Magic Eye in a
special place where other
brothers would be, where

these other brothers would
find the Magic Eye. So,
they did. They came to our
world, and to this city.
They came to this street,
because they knew two
brothers would sit on this
bench, and the two brothers
would be the special kind,
the ones who are one person.
They left the Magic Eye here
for you to find so we can
always be together, even
when I can't give you hugs,
buy you p'zzbread, and run
my fingers through your
hair.

Jo'n reaches up, catching his brother's
pale blond hair with his fingers, ruffling
Rezalton's hair.

> JO'N (CONT'D)
> Will you keep this Magic Eye
> for me so I can always be
> with you? I'm the brother
> who has to go away, Rom'n.
> I am you. We're the same
> person, you and me. As long
> as you have this Magic Eye
> with you, I'll always be
> with you, no matter how long
> I'm gone.

> REZALTON
> (takes the marble, stares inside)
> But it looks like a marble.
> It even has a chip. Right
> there.

>   JO'N
> That's what makes it magic,
> Rom'n. It looks like a
> marble to everyone except
> the brothers who use it. It
> has that chip because every
> time two brothers no longer
> need it, they get to keep
> one tiny chip to always
> remember the magic man.
> When we no longer need it,
> we will take a chip, then
> pass the Magic Eye on. Will
> you keep this with you
> always, little bro, just for
> me?

Rezalton throws his arms around his big
brother's neck, squeezing Jo'n as hard as
he can.

>   REZALTON
> I'll always keep the Magic
> Eye, Jo'n. Always. You can
> see me any time you want.
> We'll always be together.

Jo'n's eyes are closed as tears flow down
his face.

EXT. PLANET'S SURFACE - DAY (EIGHTEEN
MONTHS LATER)

Dust fills the air all the way to the
distant horizon. The landscape is
desolate. In the distance, mighty
transport landers descend straight down,
dust flying from underneath as their
shimmering repulsor screens drive the dust
into the air, finally landing on the

ground.

Troops suddenly appear through the
landers' shimmering repulsor screens.

The troops move away from the transports,
stepping through the screens. They are
clean for a moment, and then they are
immediately covered with dust, many
reaching to pull down goggles or wipe the
dust from their faces. The distant thump
of explosives fills the air.

One soldier stands out as he steps through
the repulsor screen. He stops and stands
very erect. Dirt, ash, and other floating
sediment, bits of it landing directly on
his face, suddenly assault the cleanness
of his skin.

His face vaguely resembles that of Jo'n,
only harder. The soldier's eyes flick
left and right as if assessing the
unfamiliar situation. One hand reaches up
and pulls goggles down over his eyes.

The emerging troops run directly into
waiting enclosed ground transports. Our
soldier drops into a running position and
joins the others in their dash to the
ground transport.

INT. GROUND TRANSPORT - DAY

Soldiers still in full combat dress,
already dusty and tired looking, are
sitting along the walls on benches. The
transport is basic military transportation
for a disposable military situation. It
is not old, just much used and somewhat

abused. The men jostle and shake as the transport travels along the rough ground. Most men are sitting quietly next to each other. One man, Jo'n, our soldier from the previous scene, is sitting off to himself, his attention aimed at the floor in front of him. Another soldier, GABBY, is seen looking around trying to catch someone else's eye. Gabby's eyes lock on our soldier from the previous scene. Gabby moves over next to our soldier.

Gabby speaks, his eyes still moving back and forth, his nervousness clear.

> GABBY
> Hey. This your first time, too? I've never actually been in a battle. Sim'lators, yeah, tons of times. But this is different, ya' know?

Gabby drums the tips of his shoes on the metal floor.

> GABBY (CONT'D)
> We could die here, ya' know. I mean, like, I knew that. But it was never *real*. Now it's like, right out that wall. Just reach your hand out, touch it.

Gabby leans back against the wall of the transport, his fingers doing a tap dance on his legs.

> GABBY (CONT'D)
> You, too, huh? First time?

How 'bout it?

Gabby leans over to read the pocket of the soldier's uniform.

                    GABBY (CONT'D)
          Jo'n? It is Jo'n, right? I
          don't always get names
          right, but yours is right
          there. On your shirt. They
          sure did a good job getting
          it on there nice and clear.
          I like that name. Jo'n.
          That was my best friend's
          name back before I joined
          up. Not when I was a kid,
          but from later. Nah, I
          can't become an officer like
          some of the guys. Not me.
          Didn't sign up early like
          some did. I'll just be a
          grunt, out in front for
          target practice. Hey, am I
          talking too much? The guys
          back on the ship always tell
          me I talk too much. That's
          the At'micThrust. Old-
          fashioned name, I know.
          Then, it's an old-fashioned
          ship. At least it was
          before the refit. Now it's
          good as new. The ship is,
          not the name. They kept the
          same name, At'micThrust.
          What ship did you come in
          on? Oh, dog-sheesh, I'm
          nervous.

Gabby looks over at the man with the name
Jo'n on his shirt, away, then back again,

the nervousness causing him to spasm from
time to time, his eyes suddenly opening
wide with realization. Reaching up to
brush beading sweat back from his face, he
exhales loudly.

Gabby glances at the soldier and away
again as he speaks.

           GABBY
  Oh, wow, I'm sorry, man.
  You must feel the same way.
  Hey, I'll let you be.
     (starts to stand)

Jo'n reaches up to grab Gabby's arm.

           JO'N
  Jo'n.

Jo'n looks up, his eyes flicking over in
the direction of Gabby. His face is now
clearly recognizable as the face from the
earlier scene in the city with Rezalton.
Jo'n has clearly suffered since we saw him
last. His face is thinner, and the
youthful glow is missing. He seems
lessened, as if something is missing from
his spirit.

          JO'N (CONT'D)
  My name is Jo'n. Stay.
  It'll be good to have
  someone to sit with.
  Thanks, and yeah, you do
  talk too much. What's your
  name, soldier?

           GABBY
  Gabby. Well, not really.

It's Frankl'n, but growing
up, my daddy called me that.
Kinda a girl's name I think,
but there it is. I'm used
to it. Just don't think
about it anymore, unless I'm
talking to somebody new.
Like you. The guys on the
ship thought it was pretty
funny, though. They're okay
with it now. I mean, they
don't pick on me about it so
much now. Not about that,
anyway. Uh, oh, I think I'm
doing it again, aren't I?

            JO'N
Yeah. How are ya' doing,
Gabby?

Jo'n turns to face Gabby, holding out a
hand to shake.

            GABBY
    (glancing down at Jo'n's arm)
Creepin' lime-burners! What
happened to your arm?

Jo'n traces a red, not-quite-healed scar
from his wrist to a hiding place under the
sleeve of his shirt.

            JO'N
That? That's my kid
brother.

            GABBY
Whoa, what kinda kid brother
you got? One with Krueger-
hands? I think I'd call up

the agency, get him adopted
to another *planet*.

> JO'N
>
> It ain't like that, man. My
> kid brother didn't do this
> to me. This is because he
> loves me so much. He's
> eight years old. My
> family's got some hard times
> to deal with. My brother's
> not got much. Except me.
> Of course, my parents love
> him and all. Just - when
> life's hard - you know.

Jon's fingers trace the raw scar up and
down his arm.

> JO'N (CONT'D)
>
> When I got my orders to come
> here, I had to see him.

> GABBY
>
> Hey, man. You did that?
> And they let you back in?
> In one piece?
>> (stops, understanding spreading
>> across his face)
> Not quite in one piece, huh?
> I'm sorry, man. That's
> rough.

> JO'N
>
> I'm academy trained. You
> know, signed up at thirteen.
> Graduated. Commissioned,
> and all. But I had to see
> him before I left, before I
> came here. I'm all he's

really got. You should see
him. Blond hair. White-
blond, not that brown stuff.
Skin like a ghost. Never
tans.

Jo'n holds out his hand, flat above the
floor, the red scar seeming alive as it
moves along his arm.

                JO'N (CONT'D)
About this tall. Eight when
I last saw him. Probably
nine now. With the hospital
time, and all, I've kinda
lost track. Anyway, all
that's gone. It was worth
the price, though, to see
him before I came.

                GABBY
     (shakes head)
That must be some kid
brother you've got there. I
hope he knows what a brother
he has. You guys must
really be close for you to
give up your commission and
everything, just to see him
again.

                JO'N
Yeah, you could say that.
Rom'n and me, we're pretty
close.

Jo'n holds up one hand, crossing two of
his fingers, one over the other.

                    JO'N (CONT'D)
          Just like that.

Gabby and Jo'n sit together for a few
minutes as their conversation continues,
the transport rocking, their hands
occasionally grabbing for support, Jo'n's
scar vibrant each time he does so.

EXT. BATTLEFIELD - DAY

Explosions are happening all around.
Tracers are flying from in the distance to
the foreground, the explosions throwing up
clouds of dirt and dust. The air is black
with the battle. Just dimly the sun can
be seen in the thick haze of dust and
smoke in the air. In the foreground,
soldiers are manning weaponry behind dirt
berms. They are facing away toward the
distance. Most are wearing visors over
their faces.

Gabby and Jo'n are together with visors
over their faces, lifting them and
hunkering down just before each explosion.
They attempt to talk during each lull in
the explosions.

                    GABBY
               (yelling)
          See, I told ya'. Target
          practice. Captgen'ls in the
          back, safe. Grunts to the
          front. We've made it so
          far, Jo'n. Just like the
          sim'lators. Nobody dies in
          the end. Stick with good
          ol' Gabby. You'll see.
          That kid brother of yours'll

                      136

see you again, yet.

Gabby snaps his visor down, rising to look above the dirt berm.

INTERCUT WITH THE VIEW INSIDE ONE OF THE VISORS:

A shot of the view inside the visor fills the screen. An electronic display, the enemy troops and military hardware that were invisible through the dust and smoke are now clearly seen, although it is in a representative format. Readouts for distance, troop counts, and vehicle tactical information scroll across the view. Suddenly, the arcing track of an incoming tracer begins to white out the visor.

BACK TO THE BATTLE SCENE:

Gabby flips his visor up and hunkers down. A thundering explosion sends dust billowing over Gabby and Jo'n.

Their faces are streaked with smears from dirt encrusted around mouths and ears, and their fingernails are black with the battlefield. Beneath his visor, Jo'n flashes a big grin to Gabby.

>   JO'N
>   (yelling)
>   I've got your butt covered,
>   Gabby. Just don't leave
>   mine sticking out when the
>   big one hits. Hey, man,
>   hand me that power cartridge
>   just behind you.

Gabby flips onto his stomach, reaching for
the power cartridge, and Jo'n turns back
to peer over the berm.

INTERCUT WITH VIEW FROM JO'N'S VISOR:

An incoming tracer whites out the view.

BACK TO THE BATTLE SCENE:

Jo'n flips his visor up and turns to yell
a warning to Gabby. As he does so, a
series of distant explosions drowns him
out. His mouth is yelling, but only the
explosions can be heard.

His visor still flipped up, Jo'n's eyes
cut from the incoming tracer to Gabby who
is still gathering ammunition, unaware of
the incoming mortar. In an instant,
Jo'n's face reflects understanding of what
he has to do, and his decision to act
writes itself across his face. Jo'n leaps
onto Gabby's back.

Jo'n is pressing tightly against Gabby.
Gabby turns his head. He makes eye
contact with Jo'n, a questioning look of
astonishment on Gabby's face. The sound
of the battle mutes as the ground under
the two men expands, flinging them upward.
As the men are thrown upward, Jo'n calls
out his brother's name.

EXT. BATTLE CRATER - DAY (A FEW MINUTES
LATER)

Sound returns. On the edge of the crater
formed by the explosion are Jo'n and

Gabby.

Jo'n is still on Gabby. Gabby's face is
turned upward, his eyes closed, his head
flat on the ground. Blood drips off Jo'n
onto Gabby. Gabby starts awake, flicking
his eyes to get a handle on the situation.
He notices Jo'n. In a quick motion, Gabby
rolls underneath Jo'n, catching Jo'n as he
falls off.

Gabby holds Jo'n in a hug. Gabby lifts
his hand from Jo'n's back to see blood
covering his hand.

Gabby leaps to his feet, pulling Jo'n up
with him.

>   GABBY
> I've got ya', man.

Gabby drags Jo'n with one hand under an
arm, the other holding the hole in Jo'n's
side.

Jo'n starts and coughs. Gabby stops to
look at him. Blood runs from Jo'n's mouth
with Jo'n obviously trying to talk.

>   GABBY
> What Jo'n? What do you want
> to say?
>   (leans head in close)

>   JO'N
> I knew I wasn't going home.
> Even before I came. My
> brother . . . if you make
> it, Gabby, send my things to
> him. The place. My home.

You'll find the place in my
things, Gabby.
          (the final words bubbling from
          Jo'n's lips)
You've been a friend to me,
Gabby. A good friend.

Jo'n's head is on Gabby's chest, his eyes
open, obviously dead. Tears trace a path
through the dirt on Gabby's face.

INT. REZALTON'S CHILDHOOD BED - NIGHT

A sharp crack as of overheated glass that
can no longer take the strain wakes
Rezalton. Rezalton, age 8-9, sits up in
bed. He reaches above his bed to take
something from the rafter.

Rezalton's hand is holding the marble he
found in the street in an earlier scene.
He wraps his fingers around the marble.

Rezalton snuggles back under the
bedclothes when suddenly he sits again,
throwing the covers aside. He inspects
the marble, holding it up to the dim light
coming in through an open window. His
body droops as if understanding something
he does not want to know. He then reaches
up on the rafter, feels around a bit, and
brings down something else.

Rezalton's fingers are holding a small
chip from the marble. He looks down, then
tears start in his eyes.

Rezalton lies on his bed, the tears now
running from his eyes.

ACT XI - THE HAZING

INT. MEGACORP SHIPBOARD GYM - NIGHT

BOFSKY, age thirteen, is in his
undershorts, running, apparently enduring
an academy hazing. Bofsky's bare chest is
just starting to reflect upcoming manhood.
His skin is sweaty, and he is panting with
exhaustion. Bofsky squeezes his eyes
tightly over and over as if trying very
hard to keep awake. An UPPERCADET VOICE
calls out to him.

                 UPPERCADET VOICE
      Hey, newbie. You can slow
      down. Stop, even. The run
      is over. It sure looks good
      for you. You passed all the
      others and came in first.
      That's some good form,
      there.

A strong hand slaps Bofsky on his sweaty
shoulder, and Bofsky heads towards the
corridor.

                 UPPERCADET VOICE (CONT'D)
      Just a minute, newbie.

Giving up, already? We've
got more competitions.
You've made a good start,
but you haven't proven
yourself, yet. If you want
to stay, get back with the
others.

A look of dismay crosses Bofsky's face as
he turns, still panting. He looks to see
other newbies standing around. Many are
leaning over, hands on knees, panting.
Others are sitting, rolling their heads to
relieve stiff necks. A few are rubbing
sleepy eyes.

              UPPERCADET VOICE (CONT'D)
   (loudly)
The hang is next. The rings
are on the wall. Each
newbie has to grab two of
the rings and hang there for
as long as possible. The
first to fall down can try
to pull as many others down
as possible. The last one
wins and is finished.
Here's the catch. Only one
wins each time. Once the
last person wins, everyone
goes up on the rings, and it
starts again. You must win
to be good enough to be a
cadet. Play to win.
Everybody ready?

Newbies reach to grab the rings, some
hanging and falling, with occasional
cheering by the older cadets for the
isolated winner. Bofsky only hangs each

time for a minute, then drops and pulls
the weaker participants down, even getting
the little ones to pull other little ones
down. Panic grows on faces as newbies try
to hang on despite being pulled from the
rings by Bofsky's encouragements. Soon,
most of the biggest kids have already won
their matches. Bofsky now clearly towers
over the remaining newbies. When Bofsky
chooses to go for his win, he does so
easily.

INT. BOFSKY'S BUNK - NIGHT

Bofsky climbs into his bunk. He places
his face on his pillow, clearly exhausted
and glad to be back in bed. Almost
immediately the shriek of the wakeup bells
and the lights flashing to full brightness
assault him.

>   GROWNUP VOICE
>   All out! Ten minutes to roll
>   call. Today we try for our
>   skill levels. Be thankful
>   for a good night's rest. It
>   will be the last one for a
>   good, long time.

Bofsky grimaces. A pair of legs drop down
from the bunk above Bofsky, the feet
pivoting up and down and the toes
stretching wide then relaxing. Bofsky
throws back his blanket and sits up,
rubbing his face with one hand, the other
reaching across his stomach and scratching
his side.

INT. CORRIDOR - DAY (SEVERAL WEEKS LATER)

Bofsky walks down a corridor past a closed utility door. A sign clearly labels the door. UTILITY. In smaller letters underneath are the words RESTRICTED ACCESS. Bofsky walks past the door and then stops.

Bofsky's brow bunches in puzzlement as he cuts his eyes to the door behind him. He steps back and reaches his hand to grab the doorknob.

Bofsky presses his ear to the door. Muffled sounds of someone being beaten are heard. He slowly twists the knob, and a surprised look crosses his face when the door pops open a few inches.

Bofsky steps through the door, glancing both ways in the outside corridor to make sure he hasn't been seen entering the utility corridor. Utility items are all along the corridor, including pipes, sharp metal plates, heat diffusers, and lighted control boxes. Bofsky steps into the morass, listening intently as the sounds grow more distinct.

INTERCUT FLASHES OF MEMORY WITH BOFSKY'S MOVEMENTS:

Just after Bofsky enters the corridor, and then as he walks further with the sounds getting louder, the memories flash by faster and faster. A puppy lying in the mud. His mother on the floor, the *man* on top of her. Credits, grabbing at them. Being pushed into the dark room. Hands on his body, taking what is his. The big man with the shovel, his mother fighting for

her son. The showers, the boys, kicking
and kicking. His knife being taken.

Bofsky finally comes to a tangle of pipes
he can just see through, but glimpses
only. He sees faces of older boys, ones
he recognizes. These are younger versions
of the three friends, Renhant, Jer'son,
and Barn't, from earlier.

Bofsky stands as the sounds and the
shadowy images of the beating go on and
on, until only the soft sounds of someone
crying in pain finally remain. After the
big boys are gone, Bofsky continues to
stand there listening to the crying, a
look of satisfaction on his face.

INT. CORRIDOR WALL - DAY (NEXT DAY)

Bofsky is attempting to peer around a
corner without being seen. The corridor
seems to be empty except for Bofsky and
the group he is attempting to watch. The
boys are the ones Bofsky recognized in the
previous scene as they tormented a newbie.
They are doing so again with a different
boy, this time in an out-of-the-way
corridor. This newbie is angry and
crying, unable to do anything, with the
bigger boys hitting on him. Renhant,
Jer'son, and Barn't laugh, then during a
long glimpse, Bofsky sees the newbie fall
down. Finally, the older boys walk away.

When the three tormentors walk away from
the newbie, Bofsky whirls around to slam
his back against the wall. His face is
flushed, and he is breathing very hard and
fast. His eyes flick towards the corner

and the newbie he can still hear crying.
Bofsky's head turns to look around the
corner once again.

Suddenly, Bofsky scrambles, almost
falling, running full speed down the
corridor. He stops at the newbie's side.
The newbie looks very young, a very sweet
thirteen, just a child, really. Tears are
in his eyes, and blood runs from his nose.
He looks up pleadingly at Bofsky.

Bofsky tenses, brings his leg back, and
kicks the newbie in the side. Then,
Bofsky turns and runs down a different
corridor, finally turning a corner. He
stops and leans against the wall.

Bofsky pants with the exertion of running.
His excitement in having kicked the newbie
is evident in the smile on his face, the
flushed look on his cheeks, and the bright
look in his eyes. The muscles in one arm
unconsciously flex, tighten, and relax
over and over. Bofsky's hand kneads the
fabric of his trousers just to the side of
his crotch. His stomach under his shirt
tightens repeatedly showing his breathing
increasing rapidly in speed. His hand
kneads his trousers faster and faster.

LATER:

INT. BOFSKY'S BUNK - DAY

Bofsky is standing at his open locker. A
change in shadow and a subtle shift in
background noise cause Bofsky to freeze.
He turns to look over his shoulder.

                    JER'SON
          Guys, it's the fan club.

Bofsky turns further and sees Renhant and
Barn't with Jer'son. Jer'son laughs,
grabbing Bofsky's hand to shake.

                    JER'SON (CONT'D)
          We saw you with that newbie.
          Good going. Too bad he
          didn't have any credits.
          Sometimes they do. Want to
          be at our next planning
          meeting? Ha!

Jer'son looks at the others, laughs, and
shakes his head at them, obvious in his
disdain for his own words.

                    JER'SON (CONT'D)
          All we ever plan is how to
          get credits from another
          newbie. Barn't here filched
          a code to that utility
          corridor. Yeah, we saw you
          in there. We waited to see
          what you'd do. You didn't
          tell. You seem okay. We
          meet in there, in the
          utility corridor. By the
          way, I'm Jer'son, and this
          is Renhant.

Bofsky relaxes and grins warmly, his eyes
moving to each of the three boys, resting
on each in turn.

INT. BOFSKY'S BUNK - DAY (SEVERAL WEEKS
LATER)

                    147

All four boys sit on Bofsky's bunk.
Bofsky is sitting cross-legged, another of
the boys next to him. The last two are
sitting on the ends, leaning in, one with
an arm out to brace himself on the bed,
the other holding a paper credit.

>   BOFSKY
> Here.

Bofsky slaps a wad of paper credits on the
bunk.

>   BOFSKY (CONT'D)
> What have you others got?

Each of the boys hands over a wad of
credits. They watch eagerly as Bofsky
counts and divides the stack into four
piles. Handing one wad to each of the
boys, Bofsky smiles.

>   BOFSKY
> Just a little organization,
> boys. Now look at how well
> we're doing. This is great,
> taking from the newbies,
> giving to the needy - us!
>   (guffaws)
> Ready for a game? A good
> bet is the only game in
> town.

A pile of unusual-looking cubes is on the
bunk in four jumbled piles. Each of the
four boys reaches in, and only those cubes
that belong to that particular boy jump
into the air below his palm. Each boy
shakes his open palm, and the floating
cubes rock and spin. Each boy flicks his

hand forward, making a fist as he does so, causing the cubes to fly off to the bunk below. There are both groans and sounds of excitement.

                    BARN'T
         Okay, Renhant.   Cough up.

Bofsky and Jer'son laugh.

ACT XII - THE BRINGER OF NEWS

EXT. REJUVENANT/SE'YAN'T - DAY

The time is the recent past. RJORCK is
looking into the distance across a blue
sea. Dual suns are low on the left and
right horizons. His face shows strain,
and then we see him take a deep breath, a
smile crossing his face. He glances
around, seeming pleased.

Rjorck kneels. He dips a hand into the
water, laughing to himself as his hand
disappears then reappears as he pulls it
out again. Rjorck starts to stand.

Ripples appear in the water, approaching,
indicating something just under the
surface. Rjorck looks at the ripples,
anticipation on his face.

The water in front of him mounds up.
ADHOR'K appears only as the water peels
from her, revealing a youthful, glowing
beauty. The water reveals her bare
shoulders and back, her long hair dripping
water in rivulets.

Rjorck pulls a folded cloak from under his tunic, undrapes it, and hands it to Adhor'k. There is a slight pause before she accepts it.

Adhor'k slips the cloak around her shoulders. Her right hand reaches under her hair and flips her long hair out from inside the cloak, letting it fall down her back.

Adhor'k's eyes are cast demurely down. She raises them to look directly at Rjorck as she speaks.

> ADHOR'K
> Thank you, Brother. I had hoped your ship would be in before it was time for me to return.
> (pause)
> I have heard many whispers during my sojourn. Others in the c'habor-reneis't shared their hyr'yan't with the waters. I feared for my memories of you. C'storr, Berian, and Wolmn were present at my ceremony. Others were not, but it was you I most missed.

Adhor'k reaches out and touches Rjorck's shoulder.

> ADHOR'K (CONT'D)
> You must swim with me. Your time will be soon. Your years weigh heavily on you. I can see them in your eyes.

                    RJORCK
          (deep breath and pause)
     You alone lift my burden,
     Adhor'k. My sister.

Rjorck and Adhor'k walk down the rocky
beach, the wind blowing their robes.
Adhor'k's hair is dry and blowing in the
wind. Rjorck cradles Adhor'k's elbow in
his hand. He leans to her, speaking
earnestly.

                    RJORCK
     Our people are in danger.

Rjorck continually watches his feet as if
finding his way among the stones on the
shore.

                    RJORCK (CONT'D)
     An Earth corporation has
     pointed inquiries in our
     direction. I have worked
     many years to quash rumors
     and deflect interest, but
     suspicions will no longer be
     ignored.

Rjorck reaches out, pausing, resting his
hand on a large, black boulder.

                    RJORCK
     I still have time before my
     c'habor-reneis't. I have
     grown to love that place
     they call Earth. But for
     needing to share my
     concerns, I would have
     stayed longer.

Rjorck and Adhor'k continue down the
shore. Adhor'k repeatedly takes steps and
stops, a pensive look on her face.

                    ADHOR'K
          We are all aware - and
          grateful - for your
          affection for your home-
          away-from-home, favorite
          brother. How else could you
          bear spending so many years
          away?

Adhor'k pauses and grabs Rjorck's arm,
stopping him. Rjorck turns to her.

                    ADHOR'K (CONT'D)
               (voice hard)
          But these suspicions? How
          can there be suspicions?
          They cannot know, cannot
          prove what we have never
          shared. This is our world,
          our way. They have all they
          desire and do not need
          anything from us.

INTERCUT:

EXT. STONE ON THE BEACH - DAY

A stone rests on the beach, water lapping
its edges, and then falling away.
Rjorck's hand comes into view caressing
the stone with his hand, rubbing his thumb
back and forth over one edge.

BACK TO RJORCK AND ADHOR'K:

Rjorck's face and eyes are downcast. His
eyes flick up to Adhor'k, one eyebrow
raised, a cheerless smile at the corner of
his mouth. After a pause, Rjorck drops
his eyes again.

                    RJORCK
               (in a near whisper)
          Humans have one thing they
          do want from us. They think
          of incredibly long lives as
          being the greatest of riches
          in the entire galaxy.
          Earth-humans have grown
          accustomed to taking what
          they want, handing out
          payment in return if
          possible, violence if
          necessary.

Rjorck's face and eyes remain downcast.

                    ADHOR'K
               (sharply)
          Violence!

Rjorck flicks his head and eyes in
Adhor'k's direction.

Adhor'k's gaze moves between Rjorck and
the sea, jerking as she speaks.

                    ADHOR'K
          We are not a violent people.
          We know only peace with our
          world and ourselves. It has
          been that way since the
          beginning of all we have
          known.

Adhor'k steels her expression, her mouth
tight, her eyes looking to the sea, the
wind pushing her hair from her face. She
stands facing the wind for a moment.

                ADHOR'K (CONT'D)
        And they cannot take what we
        cannot give.

Rjorck stands and puts his arm around
Adhor'k, facing into the wind, also.

                RJORCK
            (softly)
        Sister. Sister. They will
        try. Our people must
        prepare. We have a little
        time. But that is all. A
        little time.

Adhor'k steps away, reaching for the front
of her cloak, standing erect. She faces
the sea as she speaks.

                ADHOR'K
        Se'Yan't's waters will
        soothe you, Brother. True
        refreshing will come only in
        c'habor-reneis't, but just
        to immerse yourself. The
        water-weir to refresh
        yourself.
            (pause)
        You must miss it with your
        c'habor-reneis't so near.
        Come with me.
            (turns to look at Rjorck)
        Breathe the waters.

Adhor'k moves to the water's edge, and she

lets the cloak fall to her feet. She
turns her head to Rjorck, pleading in her
eyes.

Adhor'k steps into the water. At waist
level, she drops in, disappearing into the
clear liquid of her world's blue seas.

Rjorck stands, the setting sun glinting on
the water behind him, the dawn breaking in
his face. After a few moments of
introspection, he slips his tunic over his
head, dropping it to the stones.

Rjorck peers down at his reflection in the
water. He sees his gray hair, thickening
waist, and mottled skin. Upon seeing
this, Rjorck's face suddenly droops, his
weariness apparent in his expression. He
steps resignedly ahead, his body
disappearing as he slips beneath the
water's surface.

INT. MEGACORP BOARDROOM - DAY (ONE YEAR
EARLIER)

RJORCK, carrying his many years, stands
erect in full formal dress. He is very
old, although he carries himself with
sureness and confidence. Behind him are
tall double doors, now open, but in the
process of being closed. Through the open
doors can be glimpsed the interior of a
grand though austere corporate building.
In front of Rjorck is a long, curved table
backed by floor-to-ceiling windows.
Through the windows is a magnificent city
bustling under the brightest of days. At
the table, with their backs to the
windows, sits a row of elegant men of

various ages, all assuming a look of power
and privilege. The center chair is raised
to a higher level than the rest indicating
a position of power. Above this chair is
a huge revolving Earth with realtime
images of the world fully displayed on its
surface. Superimposed on these images are
the imposing letters M and C.

Rjorck bows his head and continues a
confrontation.

> RJORCK
> You may certainly make such
> a request. However, Grand
> Ser, I cannot express an
> equal desire to accede to
> your, eh-hem, requests.

The MAN at the raised chair leans forward,
his face flushed with sudden anger.

> FIRST MAN
> I am MegaCorp! How dare you
> not turn this information
> over to me. Humanity
> demands it! The record
> stick you hold in your hand
> has copies of each and every
> request made of Rejuvenant.
> These have been gone over by
> the very best World-lawyers
> our company can buy, signed
> off by GlobalPresident
> Benetin, and encrypted with
> enough funds to buy your
> people whole new worlds to
> inhabit. You do not have
> the right to refuse.
> (slams fist on table)

                    RJORCK
          (bowing)
     Most Honored Ser, it is my
     wish at all times to accede
     to the wishes and mandates
     imposed on me by my esteemed
     betters. If you wish to
     present a petition for
     something I am able to
     provide, I will do the
     utmost possible to grant
     your request. However, for
     those things of which I do
     not pretend to have
     knowledge, I am at a loss.
     All the legal forms, high-
     ranking initials, and
     monetary funds cannot
     purchase what I do not
     possess.
          (slight cough)

Several of the men looking on nod in
agreement as SECOND MAN takes the floor
and begins to speak.

                    SECOND MAN
          (standing)
     Councilor Rjorck, I have
     DataRecc records on file
     going back three hundred
     twenty years. Your name is
     signatory to multiple
     documents throughout this
     time span. On each of these
     signatures is your personal
     DNAuthorize stamp. Each of
     these is *exactly the same.*
     Throughout the entire three
     hundred twenty years. Do

you mean you wish to tell us
there has been more than one
Councilor Rjorck with DNA
exactly matching your own?
In our current level of
technology, we've learned to
duplicate metals such as
gold and a'tiaganon,
insubstantials such as
people's memories, and even
some lower life forms. But
there is one thing that no
company, not even MegaCorp,
can do, and that is
duplicate human DNA. Not
unless there has been a
breakthrough that not even
our World-lawyers are aware
of. Spare us this farce,
Councilor.
        (glaring, slams DateRecc on table)

As Rjorck begins to speak, the faces
around the table reflect disbelief at the
mildest, fury at the worst.

                RJORCK
Dear Munificent Ser, my life
is as you see it. I am no
longer a young man. How can
the years be rerun so they
can be lived again? Can an
old man such as myself
extend his reach into the
future? Can I live today
yet keep my hand on the
distant past? I am
unfamiliar with your files
and records, how they are
kept and what they record.

I am only a humble
councilor. My DNAuthorize
stamp is mine; I will own
that without question. But
to have been in use by me
for over three centuries?
Surely you jest, Worthy Ser.
Such a thing could not be
possible. Surely, if you
will search your files,
there has been an error in
record keeping. Perhaps a
glitch in transcribing, a
faulty data plate, or a
power surge. Rjorck is not
an uncommon name. I share
it with many other people.
Please, Ser, understand that
all I have is yours. But
this, this is something I do
not have. Your request
astounds me.

SECOND MAN
This world of yours is far,
Councilor Rjorck. Travel
outside the inner systems is
slow. But MegaCorp's reach
is long. We have the
authorization. No one will
stop us. You are not the
only resident of Rejuvenant.
Someone there will tell what
we wish to know. If we have
to pluck each and every
living being from the face
of that planet, we will know
the truth behind what we've
uncovered. Humanity *demands*
it. Look around you.

Billions of people die each year. How many of those billions will stand up to defend your planet when they know their very *existence* is being snuffed out, and *you could prevent that?* You have time, Councilor. Time to tell us what we wish, no, *demand* to know! You have time. For now. But that time will run out. MegaCorp will have its answers. Humanity will have its answers. Do you have anything to say?

Rjorck looks up and down the table, the expression of hope on his face fading, as no one seems to offer any hope of support.

          RJORCK
Privileged Sers, your power is great, and my ability is poor. I will pray to the gods beneath us that you will find wisdom.

Rjorck bows graciously. He backs out of the room, only turning to stride quickly down the hall once the great double doors have closed completely.

INT. RJORCK'S SUITE OF APARTMENTS - DAY

MONTAGE:

Rjorck is seen at a 'glass' data unit, scheduling travel to his home world of Rejuvenant/Se'Yan't.

Rjorck is quickly packing his most
treasured possessions and readying himself
for a long journey.

Rjorck picks up a fresh lemon from a bowl,
looking at it longingly.

Rjorck stands at full-length windows,
looking out into a single setting sun, his
face red in the oncoming sunset.

ACT XIII - THE MAGIC MAN

EXT. STORMY RIDGE - NIGHT (MILLENNIA AGO)

In the distance is a lone, leafless tree
on a ridge, illuminated by flashes of
lightning. Rain pelts the grass.

Something under the tree is moving. It
appears to have horns yet walk on two
feet. Suddenly, something large falls
from the tree, and the horned apparition
trudges down the ridge, continuing to be
illuminated by the continuous lightning.

EXT. HUT EXTERIOR - NIGHT

The horned apparition, the MAGIC MAN from
an earlier scene, is seen as little more
than a shadow as he approaches the hut's
door. With a tall staff, the door is
pushed open, the glowing flames of a fire
seen inside.

Out walks a youth, no more than fourteen,
although clearly past puberty. He wears
only a backless loincloth with a strip of
leather tied up over one shoulder. His
hair is shoulder length and braided into

several loose bunches. The wail of a
distraught woman is heard through the open
hut door.

> MAGIC MAN
> (with forced bravado)
> Come, boy. It's time.

The apparition slips a cord over the
youth's head, and the glow of an attached
glass bead with flames inside are seen in
the light from the open hut door.

EXT. PATH - NIGHT

The boy and the apparition walk down a
trail, illuminated by the flashes of
lightning. In the distance are the dim
outlines of village huts with a huge
bonfire blazing. The path of the boy and
the apparition clearly lead them there.

EXT. VILLAGE - NIGHT

The bonfire just to its side brightly
lights a hut. A number of village men are
standing back, visible in the light of the
flames, unwilling to draw close to the
hut. Piles of logs are near the bonfire,
and two men are throwing one on the
flames.

The horned apparition and the youth come
into the light. At the door to the hut,
the boy turns to face the apparition, and
this time, with a visible human hand, the
apparition reaches up to the glass bead at
the boy's neck.

                    MAGIC MAN
          Be strong, my child.

                    BOY
          (with a quaver in his voice)
          Will it hurt? Much?

The apparition wraps its hand around the
bead, reaches its other hand up to place
it on the boy's shoulder, and stands for a
moment. The apparition gives the boy a
quick hug and backs away.

                    MAGIC MAN
          The gods will be your strength.

The cloth at the hut's door is pulled
aside, and in the glow of the firelight,
numerous hands reach to pull the boy into
the hut.

INT. HUT - NIGHT

MONTAGE:

It is dark in the hut. In the dim light
reflecting from moist skin are several
village girls, more women than girls, but
obviously very young.

The boy is helped onto a raised mat.

A thick grease is worked into the boy's
hair.

Glimpses of his skin being oiled with
caressing strokes are seen.

The glass bead around the boy's neck, its
importance not escaping us, is repeatedly

shown. Each time, the glow of the flames
is visible inside.

EXT. BONFIRE - NIGHT

The bonfire still burns brightly, but the
pile of logs is significantly smaller.
Several of the men are sitting and dozing.
It is clear several hours have passed
since the boy entered the hut.

BACK TO INTERIOR OF HUT:

The boy lies on the mat exhausted, the
girls sitting around him petting his arms
and legs, feeding him pieces of fermented
fruit.

BACK TO BONFIRE:

The village men throw an additional log on
the fire. The storm continues. Out of
the hut walks the boy, alone. He stands
in the firelight, a drugged expression on
his face.

The horned apparition steps up to the boy,
grasps the glass bead still around the
boy's neck, then releases it, placing its
hand against the boy's chest, pressing the
bead into the boy's skin. The glass bead
glows in the darkness, the flames of the
fire seen inside. The apparition steps
away as the village men take the boy by
the hand, walking him toward the bonfire.

The oil on the boy's skin reflects the
flames of the bonfire itself. The boy
forces his eyes open, glances at the storm
overhead, then squints with a sigh of

resigned acceptance.

EXT. RIDGE - DAWN

The sun is rising, and the sea fractures
the dawn across the ridge. Atop the ridge
is the leafless tree. Something is
swinging from a high branch. The horned
apparition is visible silhouetted against
the brightening dawn sky.

The surf pounds in the background. On the
ground, pulled down the day before, are
the remains of a sheep's head and other
animal parts stuffed into cloth sewn and
tied to simulate the shape of a man.

The shape in the tree is a lightly charred
form, manlike, hanging from the feet, tied
to the largest branch in the tree. It
swings in the fresh morning breeze coming
off the ocean. As the sunlight hits the
thing swinging in the tree, something
catches the sun's rays and reveals a glass
bead tied with a leather cord hanging from
the neck. The bead is now clear, all the
fire gone.

The recognizable facial features are those
of the boy.

The apparition stands under the tree. To
one side is the sea, and to the other are
the green mountains plummeting toward the
water. Two human hands pull a bag out of
its robes, pouring the contents into one
of the hands.

The apparition's hands open to reveal a
dozen glass beads each about the size of a

marble. The hands roll them around as the
beads flash with flames, ice, and other
images. The hands slip the glass beads
back into the bag and place them back
inside the apparition's robes.

The apparition then reaches both hands up
to its horns and lifts them off, revealing
a very real, very weathered man. Tears
flow down his cheeks as he shakes his
head, turns, and begins to walk down the
hill.

The body of the boy swings in the tree as
the old man walks down from the ridge.
The surf sounds. The wind whistles. The
boy's body continues to swing as the rays
of the morning sun glow on his body,
turning him red with the early morning
dawn.

ACT XIV – THE BIG MAN AS MONSTER

EXT. RAMPAGING STORM – NIGHT (MILLENNIA LATER)

MONTAGE:

Total darkness is broken by brilliantly lit scenes of a violently destructive storm. With each image, the rippling crash of thunder resonates.

Lightning laces the clouds and/or strikes the ground.

A small boy, clearly recognizable as Bofsky, perhaps four, is huddled with his arms wrapped around a small dog, both of them in the storm in a semi-protected spot. The rain splatters them when the wind whips it over them.

A burly, rough-looking man is searching for something or someone.

The boy cringes each time he catches the sound of the man's voice over the fury of the storm.

A VOICE OVER is heard throughout this series of scenes, the cryptic poetry coinciding with the scenes and the fury of the storm. There is a pregnant pause between the narrations of each poem.

          NARRATOR (VOICE OVER)
    (POEM 1)
Color melts,
Sliding through my thoughts.

The blackness of the walls
Turns to sadness.

My heart breaks.

I am alone.
    (POEM 2)
Lightning
Strikes at my heart,
Burning.

I turn,
The pain
There on my face.
You turn away.

You do not see
Me cry.
My heart

Bleeds.
    (POEM 3)
Pain.
Searing, hot.

Run, the hiding
Is gone.

Emptiness
Is all.
   (POEM 4)
Darkness
Cannot hide
The hurt
We bear.

Its tearing
Pain
Is all we
Know.

We cry.
No one hears.
   (POEM 5)
You look at me,
A knife slicing my
compassion.

My soul bleeds.
Its salve is unnoticed.

I reach out.
You strike.

You are unforgiven.

INT. COTTAGE - NIGHT

The room is well worn and roughly
furnished. A roughly made door flies
open. A poorly dressed WOMAN with pale
skin and black hair jumps as the sound
startles her. She is a younger version of
Bofsky's mother killed in an earlier
scene. She carries the remains of
extraordinary beauty, but the scars and
bruises of her life with the BIG MAN have
stolen much of it from her.

The storm raging just outside comes
through the opened door, the water blowing
into the room onto the floor's rough
planking.

The big man steps inside, huge against the
low ceiling.

> BIG MAN
> Curse that boy!
> (walks forward)
> And curse that dog!
> (shakes fist at ceiling)
> That goes for this storm-
> cursed planet with its black
> skies and crop-eating
> storms!

The big man sinks into a chair near the
woman. Empty containers of strong drink
litter the area.

The big man grabs one of the containers
with liquid still inside and takes a long
swig. He growls to himself.

> BIG MAN (CONT'D)
> (muttering)
> He will not live through the
> night this time, no matter
> what that woman says.

A smirk of satisfaction grows on the man's
face as he finishes his words.

Suddenly, the big man stands, towering
over the woman. He reaches a big hand out
and grabs the front of the woman's dress,
roughly slamming her back into the wall.

As her head droops, the smear of her blood
appears on the wall.

                    BIG MAN
          I will have that strop. And
          that strop will have that
          boy. Mind you, that dog
          will get even worse.

The big man flings the woman to the floor,
snarling as he grabs a metal cup of drink
and pours more inside before putting it to
his mouth.

                    BIG MAN (CONT'D)
          You try to get in my way
          again, woman, and that strop
          will come for you, too.

                    WOMAN
               (sobbing)
          Willane. Oh, my poor
          Willane.

The woman huddles in the dimness of her
corner, one hand holding her matted hair,
the other wiping the flood of tears.

The big man staggers drunkenly as he
rifles through the room. The woman draws
further into the corner as he speaks
again.

                    BIG MAN
          When I get back, I'll have
          you, woman.
               (throws head back and laughs)
          You'll be just the thing to
          sate my appetite after I
          finish with that pup of

yours, him and that dog.

The big man pulls a chest from a wall, and
he retrieves the hidden strop. He shakes
it in her direction.

> BIG MAN (CONT'D)
> Hiding it from me, were you!
> I knew it when it went
> missing. You, taking sides
> with that boy. I'll take an
> extra little morsel of you
> tonight. Just you wait,
> woman. Just you wait and
> see.

The big man stumbles back outside into the
storm.

EXT. RAMPAGING STORM - NIGHT

The lightning tears apart the sky, giving
glimpses of the action. A few spoken
words are heard in the silence.

> SMALL BOY
> (to dog)
> I promised to keep you safe.
> I can't. Not from him.

The big man's hand pulls the boy from his
hiding spot, yanking the dog out of the
small boy's grasp.

> SMALL BOY (CONT'D)
> No! He's mine!

The big man kicks the small boy into the
mud, holding the dog, no longer
struggling, by the neck high in the air.

                    BIG MAN
            (spits out angrily)
        You want the dog, do you?
        Go get it!

In one flash of lightning, the big man
flings the seemingly lifeless dog into the
blinding rain. The small boy scrambles to
his feet to go to the dog.

Suddenly, the boy drops face down as the
big man slams the strop across his back.
The small boy curls into the mud, his
fetal position his only protection against
the beating. The beating continues, lit
only by flashes of lightning, during the
following voiceover.

                NARRATOR (VOICE OVER)
            (POEM 6)
        Hear the wind,
        Keening fingers reaching
        deep inside,
        Hungry for what we will not
        give.

        Takes.

        Wails of agony
        Etch the souls of men,
        Bleeding into the blackness.

        Crushes.

        Thunders echo
        The pounding in our blood.
        Grief unites us in passion.

        Bestows.

                    175

Wails of agony,
Hungry for that we would
give.
We hold our passion.

Hear the wind.

Lightning is followed by a final crash of thunder.

INT. COTTAGE - NIGHT

The door bursts open, puddles of rain soaking the floor as the big man carries a bundle inside.

The big man stomps to the woman still cowering in her corner. He dumps the bundle at her feet. The bundle unrolls into the small boy, badly beaten and bleeding. As the woman reaches for the boy, the big man roughly grabs her arm.

             BIG MAN
        (growling)
    This is my time, not his.
    Come to me, woman. I expect
    you to at least act like you
    enjoy this. I certainly
    intend to.

The big man rips her clothing, flinging her to the floor next to the small boy. He unties his own breeches, then falls on her.

The big man's boots, still on his feet, smear the boy's blood across the floor as the big man moves back and forth in his rape of the woman.

ACT XV - FRIENDS WON AND LOST

INT. TRANSPORT SHUTTLE - DAY

The interior of the shuttle is quite
large. It is divided into several
different spaces. Several of these spaces
have glassine walls to view the outside.
There are seats scattered against the
walls in several of the spaces. The walls
and floors are slick and smooth. Four
boys about thirteen are together. One is
REZALTON at thirteen years old, and facing
him there are three others. The largest
of these, the BOY ON SHUTTLE, grabs
Rezalton's duffel and dumps the contents
to the floor.

                BOY ON SHUTTLE
     I know you, who you are.
     You're Rezalton's brother,
     the deserter's brother.
     Hey, guys, I bet he doesn't
     even get as far as the
     toilet before he runs home
     to his mama. Ha, ha!

Rezalton reaches for his duffel, and one
of the boys kicks him in the face as he

scatters Rezalton's things across the
floor. When the things scatter, the
marble rolls away unseen. The boys tire
of Rezalton and scatter.

Rezalton pulls his duffel to himself,
wiping the blood from his nose. He looks
up at the other boys longingly despite
their cruelty. He replaces his items into
the duffel, searching for the marble for a
time before giving up. He finds and holds
the carved shell protectively.

Rezalton opens the shell and touches the
glass chip inside. He closes his eyes and
takes a deep breath, holding it, then
exhales. Then, he places the shell back
in the duffel. We hear a voice, the
speaker unseen. It is SIL'NOV, first
mentioned in an earlier scene, but not
actually seen until now.

     SIL'NOV (Off Screen)
  I'm sorry for what those
  guys did.

Rezalton cringes at the unexpected sound.
He looks up and sees the voice doesn't
belong to one of the earlier boys. Relief
floods across his features.

Sil'nov is tall and slender like Rezalton,
but dark to Rezalton's light, similar to
his brother, Jo'n.

     SIL'NOV
  They picked on the other
  singles, too. The team
  leaders shouldn't leave us
  in here alone. They think

we need to 'sort it out,'
whatever that means. I
think it's stupid. We're
kids. I guess you're
thirteen like me.

                REZALTON
Yesterday. My birthday was
yesterday. You're the only
one who knows.

                SIL'NOV
        (glancing at REZALTON from the
        corner of his eye)
They know. Trust me. They
know. By the way, my name
is Sil'nov. Like the city.
My parents did that. Just
one name, too. Weird. But,
then you have to know my
parents. That's why I
signed up. Maybe I can just
leave the weird behind.
What's your name?

                REZALTON
Rom'n. Can I be with you?
When we get there?
        (carries duffel next to Sil'nov's
        seat)

                SIL'NOV
Sure thing. You bet.
Consider it done. Those
boys give you any more
trouble, we'll take care of
'em. Together. Nobody'll
mess with us. Sil'nov and
Rom'n.
        (rolling the names around in his

mouth)
      Sil'nov and Rom'n. Hey, it
      even sounds good together.

Sil'nov puts his arm around Rezalton's
shoulder, leading him up to the glassine
clearwall. The other boys step out of
their way.

INT. DESK - DAY

A MAN sits behind a desk. Recruits are
lined up getting bunk assignment numbers.
Sil'nov and Rezalton are next in line. As
they move up, the man turns his attention
to them, handing them a tag.

                    MAN BEHIND DESK
      Got it? 42a and 42b. You
      can decide who's on top.
      Take this tag. The bunk
      numbers are printed on it
      with your names on the back.
      Slip it in the slot on the
      end of the bunk. You're
      down that green corridor,
      second door on the left.
      Mess is down the blue.
      Three units until mess call.
      Be ready or be hungry.
      Questions? No? Next!

Sil'nov and Rezalton throw their duffels
over their shoulders, looking around, very
excited and pleased to finally be on the
ship. They turn, looking up, poking each
other to point out something else they've
seen. They finally find the right
location, then run to claim the top bunk.
Sil'nov pushes Rezalton aside in a last

rush, throwing his duffel up, landing it
on the top bunk.

>   SIL'NOV
>   Mine!
>   (vaulting onto the bunk in one leap)

>   REZALTON
>   Cheater! I had it.
>   (laughs)

Rezalton steps on the bottom bunk to
playfully punch Sil'nov in the side.
Rezalton drops to the bottom bunk, raises
his feet, and kicks the bottom of the bunk
above.

>   SIL'NOV
>   Hey!
>   (drops head over side)
>   I guess I'll have to play
>   nice if I want to get any
>   sleep up here.

Sil'nov rolls off the top bunk, landing on
the floor, and he reaches to pull Rezalton
up off the bottom bunk.

>   SIL'NOV (CONT'D)
>   Let's get this tag posted
>   and get our duffels emptied.
>   See, these stor'loks beside
>   the bunks are ours.

Rezalton pulls his duffel from his bunk,
then glances from side to side at the
newbie undercadets still coming in,
locating bunks, still choosing bunkmates.
Rezalton leans to whisper to Sil'nov.

                    REZALTON
There are girls in here.
Where are they going to
sleep?

                    SIL'NOV
Sometimes I wonder what rock
you crawled out from under.
Anywhere they want. Except
in my bunk, of course.
We're not supposed to sleep
in anyone else's bunk,
especially if they're in it,
too, if you get what I mean.
But when the lights are out,
well, I've been told that
things do happen. Just not
in my bunk, thank you very
much. You can get kicked
out of the academy if they
catch you.
          (grins wickedly)
But with that face of yours,
Rom'n, you might just have
to push a few of the girls
out of your bed on those
dark, dark nights. If you
know what I mean.

Rezalton looks down and turns scarlet, as
he grabs his duffel to put his things
away.

                    REZALTON
          (quietly)
My brother was here. At the
academy. Here at MegaCorp.
He never did that, had girls
in his bed. He always did

                    182

the right thing.

Rezalton cuts his eyes to Sil'nov to make sure he hears.

INT. GYM ABOARD SHIP - NIGHT

This is a hazing. The new recruits, all about the same age, though with varying levels of physical maturity, run the perimeter of what appears to be a large though rather featureless gymnasium. In the back, several older teens monitor the younger ones.

The new recruits are dressed in identical, MegaCorp academy-issued underclothing as if they have been pulled from sleep for this activity. Both the boys and the girls are wearing white, lightweight boxer-type shorts. The girls also have loose-fitting white tops that just cover their chests. Sil'nov and Rezalton pass by. Rezalton glances around, seeming very uncomfortable in his lack of clothing. He is unable to keep his eyes off the girls around him.

LATER:

The new recruits, including those from the shuttle, are obviously very tired and sweaty, loosely lined up in a group at one side of the room.

Rezalton's eyes are cutting back and forth, suggesting he feels very uncomfortable and exposed. He keeps shifting behind Sil'nov. Sil'nov seems amused by this and keeps moving out of the way, forcing Rezalton to continually shift his position in order to use Sil'nov as a shield.

Other new recruits are standing behind Sil'nov and Rezalton, moving, leaning to speak to each other, pointing to something they want the others to see. Rezalton places his hand on Sil'nov's shoulder as Rezalton leans his head in next to Sil'nov's to whisper something in Sil'nov's ear. Sil'nov grins, looking around to see what Rezalton is talking about.

Sil'nov turns to look at Rezalton, a questioning look on his face. Rezalton is still behind Sil'nov, and he reaches his other arm around Sil'nov's neck, pointing with an outstretched arm. When Sil'nov still seems unable to find what Rezalton is talking about, Rezalton uses his free hand to grab Sil'nov's face, pointing it in the right direction. At Sil'nov's dawning recognition, Rezalton grins, ducks his head, and turns away as if to again hide behind Sil'nov.

INTERCUT:

A girl glances up, sees Rezalton pointing, and grins.

BACK TO SIL'NOV AND REZALTON:

Sil'nov and Rezalton are wrestling, each trying to get the other to look at the girl. A sound gets their attention, and both boys stand still, worried looks on their faces, as an OLDER TEEN speaks.

                    OLDER TEEN
The next test is a strength
test. Only the strongest
cadets can be part of the
MegaCorp Military Training
Arm. The weak will not be
allowed to stay. Every
newbie must take down two
other newbies. Take them
down and keep them down
until a ranked cadet can
come put a mark on your
shoulder. Every newbie must
earn at least two shoulder
marks to continue with the
tests. You must play to
win. Ready! Start!

Several of the new recruits stand looking
around, seeming unsure of what they are to
do until someone pulls them down.

Another boy suddenly jumps on Rezalton.
The boy is one of the boys from the
shuttle. The boy straddles Rezalton,
sitting on his stomach. The boy leans
into Rezalton's face.

                BOY FROM SHUTTLE
            (spitting out the words)
I know who you are,
Rezalton. *His* brother. You
really think no one would
know? *My* father told me
about what he did. Ran off.
Deserted when he was sent to
fight. Had his *commission*
stripped from him. Died a
coward's death.

                      185

Rezalton is lying on the floor. His expression goes from one of surprise to unbridled anger at the insult to his brother. His arms and chest tense, the tendons in his neck tightening, then Rezalton acts with fierceness.

Rezalton grabs one of the boy's arms, twisting and twisting. The other boy gives to dodge the pain in his arm, and Rezalton slams him down to the floor.

Rezalton drops his legs on either side of the other boy's torso, his knees in the other boy's armpits. The muscles in Rezalton's legs tense with the pressure he is putting on the other boy's torso. A hand reaches out, placing a blue mark on Rezalton's shoulder. Seeming surprised, Rezalton's attention is diverted from the boy under him, and he stands.

Rezalton's hair is sweaty, his skin is slick, and his chest is rising and falling with the exertion. His face is flushed with success. His eyes look for someone else to beat, anticipation written on his face.

Rezalton eyes another opponent and slams into them. He wrestles the new opponent, sitting on him as he had the other boy, belatedly realizing this is no boy. It is the girl from earlier. Suddenly weak, Rezalton relaxes.

The girl twists out and pins Rezalton. She stares into his face, a look of determination on her own. The mark is put on her shoulder, and she gets up.

Rezalton sits up, aware he has lost.

Rezalton breathes hard, and his eyes
follow the girl, his attention on her. He
starts and turns his head to find a second
blue mark is being placed on his shoulder.

>   REZALTON
>   (not understanding)
> Why? She beat me.

>   OLDER TEEN
>   (with a grin)
> One minute. You held her
> down one minute before she
> took you. You both win.

Rezalton sits still, his knees raised, his
arms resting on them, his chest still
heaving, and his eyes continue to search
for the girl.

INT. TRAINING SHIP DORMITORY - DAY (THE
NEXT MORNING)

Rezalton walks through the dormitory
asking the same question to repeated
people. No one seems to have an answer
for him.

>   REZALTON
> Has anyone seen Sil'nov? He
> didn't come back to his bunk
> last night.

Rezalton comes upon a girl at the end of a
row of bunks. As he leans in to ask her
his question, he reaches out and touches
her shoulder. When she turns, he
recognizes her as the girl from the night

before.

FLASHBACK (MONTAGE):

These images are quick flashes of last
night from a slightly different angle than
seen earlier.

The curve of the girl's neck.

Her panting ribcage.

Her eyes as she glances at him, then away.

His leg pressed against the curve of her
breast.

Rezalton's bare, heaving chest as seen
from his own viewpoint, the crotch of his
undershorts visible below.

The girl's legs as she walks away.

BACK TO THE DORMITORY:

Rezalton ducks his head, the redness of
embarrassment on his face. He starts to
turn away without waiting for an answer.

                    GIRL
        Hey.

At the girl's response, Rezalton turns
back to her, interest again on his face.

                    GIRL (CONT'D)
            (gently)
        I guess no one told you.
        He's in the medcenter. Last
        night, one guy refused to

give in when he didn't get
the mark, hit the guy who
did. That must be your
friend. By the way, good
job last night. Thanks for
letting me win, too. No one
else in the room did that.
You're an all-right guy.
Don't let anyone get to you
about your brother. You're
not your brother. You're
better than your brother.

Rezalton walks away down the row of bunks,
his head down, his body drooping, his eyes
filled with sudden tears of shame and
anger. The girl calls to him again.

          GIRL
Hey. Are you all right?
Hey.

INT. REZALTON'S BUNK - NIGHT

Two bunks are stacked one atop the other.
The top bunk is neatly made, empty.
Lights are out; only the glow of light
from a corridor door reveals the bunks.

Rezalton is in the bottom bunk lying on
his back, awake. A thin blanket is pulled
up to his waist. One arm is bent over his
forehead. The other is on the blanket in
his lap. His eyes look up at Sil'nov's
bunk, then he squeezes his eyes tightly,
tears leaking out.

INTERCUT:

A stilled and pasty Sil'nov lies on a

table in the medcenter. A medic reaches
to close his eyes with her fingers.
Sil'nov's face is covered by a white
sheet.

BACK TO REZALTON'S BUNK:

Rezalton's fingers are working something.
It is the glass chip from the marble.
Fabric rustles and springs creak as
Rezalton turns to his side and curls up in
a fetal position, pulling his pillow into
his arms as if for comfort in its embrace.

INT. REZALTON'S PRIVATE QUARTERS - DAY
(10 YEARS LATER)

A newly minted UnderSergeant Rom'n
Rezalton stands in front of a full-length
mirror. He is sharp in a crisp black
uniform with all the trimmings. Across
his chest is the MegaCorp logo. Next to
him stands UnderSergeant Ma'jene Holcum,
also newly minted. Holcum brushes her
palms across the trim shoulders filling
out Rezalton's new uniform.

    HOLCUM
 Just look at you!
 UnderSergeant Rom'n
 Rezalton. Who would have
 thought? Sometimes ladies'
 man. Partner. Your new
 uniform looks mighty sharp
 on you. Feels good, too.
  (laughs)
 How do I look?

Holcum steps back, pulling the hem of her
jacket taut, showing off her newly

accentuated curves.

> REZALTON
> (grinning)
> Almost as good as me,
> Ma'jene.

His eyes caress the fit of her uniform as a grin grows on his face.

> REZALTON (CONT'D)
> I wasn't so sure eight years ago, but you and I, we've made a great team. You've watched my back, and I've watched yours.

INT. SHIP'S CORRIDOR - NIGHT

Rezalton and Holcum whirl out the door of the officer's club, obviously somewhat tipsy. They toss their special promotion passes at a recycle slot, laughing together. Holcum holds Rezalton's hand above her head as she twirls around.

> HOLCUM
> Another club, good man?

Holcum nearly falls, recovers, and then sashays on down the corridor.

> HOLCUM (CONT'D)
> Follow me, undersergeant!

Holcum's hand is up over her left shoulder beckoning Rezalton along with a wiggle of her fingers. He runs to catch up, breathing hard as he slips his arm around her waist.

                    REZALTON
Here.
    (his face brushing her hair)
Let me steady you. Wouldn't
want you to fall. Our next
appointment is just the
other side of the lift.

Down a wide corridor are several closed
signs. Several more flicker on.
Occasionally, someone staggers out of the
doorway underneath one of the signs.

Holcum leans back against the corridor
wall for support. She is trim and very
alluring in her black uniform. Rezalton
leans over her, one hand on the wall, the
other in her hair. He inhales the scent
of her hair. He pulls close to her as he
brushes his face in her hair.

His lips barely move as he whispers to
Holcum.

                    REZALTON
Ma'jene. You and me. We're
a team, aren't we? *Aren't*
we? Ma'jene, I want you.

Rezalton runs the edge of his lip down the
outside of her ear.

                    HOLCUM
Rom'n, my boy.
    (rests her hands on his hips)
We will always be a team. We
have a history. A long
history. You'll never be
rid of me. But I'm crashed.

If you don't get me home and
leave me to sleep this off,
I might just have to spend
the night right here in this
corridor. Now, how would
that look when I was found
in the morning, partner?
We're a team. Now help your
old teammate home. You can
take care of your tos'rone
business on your own after
you get home. After all, we
were both fourteen together
at the academy. I used to
sleep under your bunk,
remember? Your private
spot? I remember many a
night when you kept yourself
entertained far into the
night all by yourself.

Holcum hiccups a drunken giggle, tapping
Rezalton on the chest with one long
finger.

        HOLCUM (CONT'D)
I'm sure you will remember
how it's done once you get
home.

Holcum slips out from under Rezalton's
arms, running one hand down the corridor
wall to steady herself as she staggers
away. Rezalton stands with his hand high
on the corridor wall. He turns his head
in the direction Holcum has gone.

Rezalton grabs his bottom lip with his
teeth, breathing in obvious, deep, shallow
breaths. We hear him murmur to no one

except himself.

>   REZALTON
> Partners, my muscled
> backside. Queen and slave
> is more like it. Gods in
> the underworld, she's
> beautiful in that uniform.
>   (steps away from the wall)
> Hold on, beautiful. Let me
> make sure you get there
> safely.

INT.   REZALTON'S PRIVATE QUARTERS - NIGHT

Around his quarters are many personal
items Rezalton has displayed. Many show
him involved with Holcum. Some are
images, while others are awards with both
their names on them. An opened locker
shows slacks neatly hung, shoes placed
underneath. The bed is recessed into its
niche, the blanket already pulled back,
the sheet below taut, the pillow waiting.
On the foot of the bed is a fresh pair of
undershorts waiting. Off screen the
shower can be heard running. The bathroom
door is open, and bright light is spilling
out. Inside, Rezalton is under the water,
his face upturned into the stream. No
steam is seen this time. He cries out.

>   REZALTON
> Gods! This water is shiking
> cold. I'm freezing!

Rezalton flips the water off and shoves
his hands under his armpits as he steps
from the shower.

> REZALTON (CONT'D)
> Shiking cold! Gods know why
> I put up with that woman!

Rezalton snaps a towel from the dispenser,
dancing with the cold as he dries off. As
he finishes, he runs the towel over his
hair one final time, leaving it damp and
sticking straight up. Then he tosses the
towel into the recycle slot as his teeth
start to chatter. His hand slaps the
light off as he exits to his room, dancing
with the cold as he slips his shorts on
and flings himself under the covers. He
laughs to himself as he pulls the thin
blanket to his chin.

> REZALTON
> (grinning)
> Jo'n, I could sure use your
> company tonight!

Rezalton slaps a panel on the wall by his
head, and the lights go down but not out.
The room is silent except for Rezalton's
breathing.

The blanket is stretched tightly over
Rezalton's form lying underneath, his feet
warring against his hands for possession,
the blanket not quite long enough to warm
both his feet and his neck.

MONTAGE:

INT. REZALTON'S QUARTERS - NIGHT

The images of Holcum and Rezalton
displayed throughout the room are seen,

195

with one after the other intercut with the
awards displaying Holcum's name next to
Rezalton's. The movements of his blanket
and sheet are heard off screen. After a
moment, he cries out.

> REZALTON (VOICE OVER)
> (breathing quickening, finally
> gasping)
> Ma' - JENE! Oh - oh - MA' -
> JENE! Ma' - jene . . .

INT. WORKSTATION - DAY (THE NEXT MORNING)

A hand slaps a package down on the
countertop as Rezalton walks into a room
filled with a series of work cubicles.

> HOLCUM
> Hey, there he is! That
> wouldn't be a *hangover* I see
> brooding in your eyes, would
> it, now?
> (laughs)
> Or maybe something else kept
> you awake after you got home
> last night!

Rezalton's face flushes, and he puts a
hand up to cover his eyes.

> REZALTON
> Ma'jene, don't. I asked
> you. You know I did.
> What's this?
> (points to the package)

> HOLCUM
> Something pretty-boy ought
> to know about, except he

won't get drunk with me
often enough. Go take
those. Your head will be
good as new in a matter of
minutes.

Holcum presses the package into Rezalton's
hand, leaning in so only he can hear.

                    HOLCUM (CONT'D)
          And I do like that pretty
          face of yours. Stick by my
          side, and I may just take
          you up on that offer,
          friend.

Holcum pushes him in the direction of the
nearest cleaning cubicle.

Rezalton steps into the cleaning cubicle
and sets the package on the counter,
forgotten. He leans his head against the
wall, his eyes closed. He smiles and
mouths the words Holcum just said to him.

                    REZALTON
          I may just take you up on
          that offer.

INT. T404TRAINER COCKPIT - DAY

Rezalton and Holcum sit side by side in
the cockpit of a T404Trainer pocket
lander. The bulbous glassine view walls
in front of them show the ship is being
buffeted with the heavy atmosphere.

                    HOLCUM
              (thick anger)
          Can it, Rom'n! I don't need

to hear what's going wrong.
I need you to *fix* it. Get
your friggin' hands on the
controls and help me out!
        (to herself)
Three friggin' nights on
this suck-up rock! What did
I do to deserve this?

Holcum turns to look at the man next to
her, and she studies him. She continues
to play the control panel skillfully even
as she studies Rezalton, a smile crossing
her lips.

MONTAGE:

A series of brief images of good times
with Rezalton.

Again looking at Rezalton, her smile
fading.

A tear falls from her eye, rolling down
her cheek.

Just a girl, memories of hunger, a broken
home, a bright light in her face, and man
after man taking her while she screams for
them to stop.

The view through the cockpit windows as
the ship clears the heavy atmosphere.

BACK TO THE T404TRAINER:

                HOLCUM
Gods, Rom'n! I thought you'd
lost your touch there.

                    REZALTON
          (placing his hand on hers)
       Just like silk.
          (turns to her and grins)

                    HOLCUM
          (softly)
       Just like silk, huh? Maybe
       that's just what I need.

EXT. PLANET'S SURFACE - DAY

MONTAGE:

Rezalton and Holcum are on the surface of
the planet. Shadows are cast by a thick
canopy of trees.

In glimpses of light and shadow, Rezalton
and Holcum are intimately involved.

The curve of Holcum's breast is shown in a
brief glimpse.

The arch of Rezalton's back is seen in
another.

Holcum's fingers trace Rezalton's spine in
yet another.

Rezalton's eyes are closed and his face
contorts with passion. As he lifts his
head in a final moment of pleasure,
Holcum's face reflects the same
sensations.

Rezalton lets out an audible breath, and
his face relaxes. He looks at Holcum's
face, and she relaxes and returns his

smile.

EXT.   PLANET'S SURFACE - NIGHT

Rezalton rolls off Holcum onto his side.
He continues to run his fingers up and
down Holcum's body, looking at her face
tenderly.

> REZALTON
> (whispering softly)
> Ma'jene, I can't believe
> these three nights. Here,
> with you. This is what I've
> always wanted. Since I
> first saw you at the
> academy. That's why I've
> done all those things you've
> asked me to, even when I
> didn't want to. Even as a
> boy, I would lie in my bunk
> through the night,
> remembering everything you'd
> said that day, what you'd
> done, how you'd looked. And
> on those days when you
> accidentally bumped my arm
> or leg, those nights were
> hardest. On those nights,
> this is what I dreamed of,
> these past three nights with
> you, Ma'jene. Every time.
> Sometimes until I couldn't
> take the pressure anymore.
> It was always about you,
> Ma'jene. In fact, after
> spending these three nights
> with you, I have something I
> have to say to you . . .

                    HOLCUM
          (her hand flashing to cover his
          mouth)
     No more, Rom'n. No more. I
     don't want to hear what you
     have to say. Just hold me.

Holcum kisses him until Rezalton is
finally too busy to remember what he
needed to tell her, their bodies starting
to move once more in an intimate embrace.

INT. UNDERGEN'L V'JORK'S QUARTERS - DAY
(THE NEXT MORNING)

Holcum is crisply done up in a fresh
uniform. She is at attention before
UNDERGEN'L V'JORK.

                    HOLCUM
          (crisply)
     UnderSergeant Holcum
     reporting, Ser!

Holcum snaps her heels together, her hand
raised in the regulation MegaCorp salute.

               UNDERGEN'L V'JORK
          (growling)
     Your partner. Where is he?
     Two down. Two up. But
     we'll take care of that
     later. You brought that
     T404Trainer up alone, I
     understand.

                    HOLCUM
     Yes, Ser!

                    UNDERGEN'L V'JORK
Very difficult to do. Quite
an accomplishment. Quite.
And your report. You have
it?

                    HOLCUM
Here, Ser!

Holcum snaps the sealed record stick from
her waistband, holding it out to the
undergen'l.

                    UNDERGEN'L V'JORK
Well done, undersergeant.
    (reaches out for the report)
Well done, indeed.
Actually, I've already
reviewed what you've put in
this and am very impressed.
Very impressed, indeed. I
wouldn't be surprised to see
a promotion for you out of
this. In fact, I think I
can assure you that
promotion will be yours
within the quarter.

                    HOLCUM
    (snaps her heels, giving another
    salute of thanks)
My appreciation, UnderGen'l
V'jork. Your trust in me is
a great honor. I will not
let you down.

                    UNDERGEN'L V'JORK
Now as far as that partner
of yours. UnderSergeant
Rezalton, is it? Picked up

                    202

by security rescue shortly
after you reported him
missing. Dereliction of
duty. Almost naked, wearing
only a pair of priv'tshorts.
Disgraceful. Then the
audacity of him to accuse
you of leaving him, taking
his uniform and sneaking
away in the night. Why,
that man should never have
had his uniform off. And
you the one who messaged for
his rescue, who may have
saved his life. Young
woman, you are the perfect
example of what MegaCorp is
all about. We need more
soldiers like you. As far
as Rezelton, he will be
further stripped . . .

V'jork grins and winks at HOLCUM, clearing
his throat.

   V'JORK (CONT'D)
. . . if it is possible to
do so any further, of his
rank.

Holcum lets out a laugh. The undergen'l
looks at her with a grin, and then we see
him laugh with her as if joining in a
private joke.

   HOLCUM
 (to herself as she turns away)
He loves me. How dare
Rom'n! How dare he!

Holcum laughs even louder.

INT. BOFSKY'S QUARTERS - DAY

Hands are manipulating information on a
'glass' data unit. They belong to BOFSKY
at age seventeen. Each duty roster or
message log that comes up is enlarged by
the hands to show Bofsky's name. Duty
times and message logs are altered.

> BOFSKY (VOICE OVER)
> I won't take the blame. I
> won't. It wasn't my fault.

Bofsky keys in an approval code, and words
appear on the 'glass.' CHANGES COMPLETED.
DO YOU WISH TO UNDO? Bofsky's hand
reaches, hovers over the yes, then in a
quick motion, triggers the no.

INT. MILITARY TRIBUNAL - DAY

Seventeen-year-old RENHANT, JER'SON and
BARN'T are under restraint. Their clothes
are disheveled and their eyes are red.
Desperation traces lines and dark circles
on their faces.

BOFSKY and several academy officers stand.
As Bofsky and the officers exit, Renhant
reaches out to grab Bofsky's arm.

> RENHANT
> (eyes wild)
> Willane, no! You know this
> isn't the way it went. What
> did you do? *Why* did you do
> this? You convinced the
> rest of us to go downside.

Jer'son and Barn't would've
jumped on any idea you threw
out. I only went because
you three were my friends.
Willane, tell them the
truth. Willane, we can all
beat this. We *could've*
beaten this. We don't
understand.

Bofsky leans in to whisper to Renhant.

> BOFSKY
> This is the way it's gotta
> be, Renhant. Someone had to
> go down. It wasn't going to
> be me. You were a good
> friend. However, that time
> has come and gone.

Bofsky's face hardens, showing disdain for
Renhant's display.

> BOFSKY (CONT'D)
> I'll be there for the
> inquiry. Just know this is
> the way it has to be.

LATER THE SAME DAY:

> ANNOUNCER
> Let the record show that
> Uppercadets Renhant, Barn't,
> and Jer'son are present for
> this inquiry regarding the
> fatal injury and death of
> Cadet Farbr d'Sen Zen'ri.
> All rise.

The three uppercadets stand in a line,

shoulders touching, as one in the
precision of their movements, and also as
one in their despair, faces of stone
masking their inner turmoil. Only the
flick of their eyes towards the traitor
and back again reveal their thinly
disguised self-control.

             ANNOUNCER (CONT'D)
     Uppercadet Willane Bard
     Bofsky, please step forward
     and state the nature of your
     accusation.

             BOFSKY
        (steps up)
     Yes, Ser. Those three over
     there . . .

LATER STILL:

All persons in the room are standing.

             ANNOUNCER
     Renhant, Barn't and Jer'son,
     this board of inquiry has
     reached a decision in this
     matter. Your actions have
     been found despicable.
     Rather than face
     consequences for a simple
     planetside escapade,
     consequences of which would
     have been stern but
     comparatively mild to what
     you now face, the three of
     you planned and executed a
     deed so reprehensible, it
     brings shame on this
     training academy. For

willfully conspiring to
entrap and injure unto death
one Fabr d'Sen Zen'ri, this
review board sentences you
to a permanent posting on
Rant. No appeal of this
decision will be permitted.
Transport to a waiting
jumpship has been arranged.
You will not return to your
quarters. You will be
escorted for immediate
boarding and transport to
your new posting.

Barn't leans over to Renhant and Jer'son.

                BARN'T
Posting, my backside.
That's MegaCorp cover-speak
for sentencing. Our life-
posting is just a life
sentence, and we're not even
allowed to tell anyone.
Shipped direct, prepackaged,
with overnight delivery.

                JER'SON
Did you see Bofsky? We may
deserve this, but Bofsky?
He's coming out of this with
hero all over him. Ancient
gods, he set all this up.
Why isn't *he* here?
    (under his breath, whispered)
He'll get his own. Just
wait. I'll see to it.
Somehow. Someday.

The three boys are escorted from the room,

and the REVIEW BOARD turns its attention
back to Bofsky.

             REVIEW BOARD
      Uppercadet Bofsky, please
      step forward. This board
      has noted your invaluable
      participation in bringing to
      light this incredible series
      of events that culminated in
      the death of Cadet Zen'ri.
      Upon completion of your time
      here at the academy, this
      board of inquiry has
      determined that you be
      offered a position on the
      starstrike class battleship
      of your choice. Do you wish
      to accept this board's
      offer?

             BOFSKY
        (hiding excitement)
      Sers, I would be honored to
      accept. Service to the
      corporation has been my
      life's goal. Thank you,
      Sers.

As Bofsky turns away, the grin of the
truly victorious dances across his face.

INT. SHIP'S CORRIDOR - DAY

This is graduation day. BOFSKY is in full
dress blacks as he steps through a doorway
into the corridor. He walks up to the
opaque glassine wall and watches it
trigger and turn clear at his presence.
Bofsky almost disappears against the

blackness of space. He leans into the
glassine to catch a glimpse of an incoming
battle cruiser.

                    BOFSKY
          I've been invisible too
          long. That's the ship I
          want. I want the captaincy.
          I will have it, too. Just
          wait and see.

Bofsky's eyes narrow as if the ship is
already his.

INT. GRADUATION RECEPTION - DAY

BOFSKY is standing alone as a grizzled OLD
MAN walks up behind him and slaps Bofsky
on the back.

                    THE OLD MAN
          Ahh, my good boy. Do come
          in, Bofsky. This is a fine
          day for this academy.
          MegaCorp will some day
          entrust the future of a
          battleship to one such as
          you, one with the makings of
          a captgen'l, for sure. No,
          you're not a captgen'l yet,
          my boy, but certainly, I
          think, within the
          foreseeable future.

                    BOFSKY
             (with control, although revolted)
          Ser. How good to see you
          again. There have been many
          simulated battle maneuvers
          since you joined us last.

May I assume you are here to
pick the best of the best?
You know better than any
other that this vessel
trains more captgen'ls than
any other in the fleet. I
happen to know that you,
Ser, in fact, trained on
this very vessel.

                THE OLD MAN
Not many people know that,
my boy. Not only has this
ship been through two
retrofits since my day, even
the name is no longer the
same. We used only number
and letter configurations in
my day. None of this
'named-for-so-and-so-suck-
up' that you see these days.
Give me the good old days,
anytime. Now take you,
Bofsky.
     (walking up and taking refreshments)
The future belongs to you.
You have proven yourself one
who can set a ship on its
end, control the rabble
serving under you, and make
a name for yourself. In
fact, I would be surprised
if you didn't become the
youngest captain of a
starstrike class in the
history of MegaCorp. Come
with me, my boy. I'll give
you some training, whip you
into the man your father
Bofsky must have hoped you'd

become. What do you say,
boy? Care to have a go
onboard?

Bofsky looks down at his hand and the
scars he still carries from all the
beatings. He speaks with difficulty and a
strained smile.

           BOFSKY
It will be an honor to serve
with one such as yourself,
CaptGen'l.

Bofsky turns away to where his words
cannot be overheard before he continues.

           BOFSKY (CONT'D)
   (grins)
Then I'll have your ship for
dessert.

INT. BATTLESHIP CONTROL CENTER — DAY (10
YEARS LATER)

Bofsky and SHR'DT, a sector-lieute'nt, are
working at 'glass' data consoles.

           SHR'DT
Hey, Bofsky. Would you look
at this?
   (taps glass)
Another one of those weird
goof-ups. This isn't like
the old man. Sixty-two
years he's been with
MegaCorp. Shik, he was in
the service even before the
jumpships. Now isn't that
one teat-sucker for you?

Imagine, not even having jumpships. In all those years, he's had a perfect record. Now, how many of these does this make? Nine that I know of. You came aboard at just the wrong time, Bofsky.

Shr'dt leans back in his chair, his hands behind his head, looking at the display on the glass.

> SHR'DT (CONT'D)
> You should have served with him during his heyday. That was a captgen'l to be reckoned with. All good times must end, I guess.
> (turning to Bofsky)
> I wonder how much longer he'll be able to hang on. He acts like it's business as usual, like nothing's wrong. Crazy old bird.

> BOFSKY
> (smirk Shr'dt can't see)
> I don't know, Shr'dt. The old man's like a father to me. I know I shouldn't, but I've been covering for him whenever I can. What else can I do? Move aside. This might be something I can fix. Let me see what I can do.

Bofsky angles the 'glass' for his eyes only and pulls a data stick from his

pocket. He slides it into the slot next
to the glass. Bofsky manipulates the
information on the glass, and then he
pulls the data stick from the slot.

> BOFSKY
> I have it all fixed, Shr'dt.
> I'm sure the old man's just
> had a bad string of luck.
> He'll even out. I know.
> All this'll soon be behind
> him.

> SHR'DT
> (walks up behind Bofsky)
> Thanks, Bofsky. The old man
> doesn't know just how lucky
> he is to have you behind
> him. His career couldn't be
> in better hands.

Shr'dt places a hand on Bofsky's shoulder,
and relief is on his face.

> BOFSKY
> (grins and glances up)
> I'll take care of him,
> Shr'dt. You can count on
> that.

Shr'dt moves aside as Bofsky stands to
leave.

> SHR'DT
> I know I can. I trust you,
> Bofsky. Thanks, again.

Bofsky grins to himself again as he steps
into the corridor, no one to hear as he
whispers.

                    BOFSKY
          But just what can you trust
          me to do? Do you know that,
          Shr'dt? Are you certain you
          know that?

INT. BOFSKY'S QUARTERS - DAY (SEVERAL
MONTHS LATER)

Bofsky is lying calmly on his bunk as
emergency lighting dances around the room.
The door bursts open to a CREWMEMBER.

                    CREWMEMBER
          Bofsky! All personnel
          updecks. Stat.

The crewmember exits quickly, leaving the
door open. Bofsky looks at a time clock
and goes back to sleep.

INT. CORRIDOR - DAY (SEVERAL HOURS LATER)

Emergency lighting is still on, and panels
are pulled out with workers leaning
inside, apparently trying to locate the
problem. Bofsky strides purposefully down
the corridor. He stops and knocks on a
door. It opens smartly. Bofsky stands at
attention until a sharp salute signals him
to action.

                    BOFSKY
          Bofsky, here. I am aware,
          as are the entire personnel
          of this battleship, of the
          dire nature of our
          predicament. However.

Bofsky turns to pointedly bore his stare
at THE OLD MAN.

> BOFSKY (CONT'D)
> Time must be made to point
> blame at the source of the
> problem. I have here in my
> hand records showing
> intentional negligence and
> willful disruption of the
> operations of this
> battleship. Not only have
> these actions been grossly
> inflicted on the personnel
> of this ship, they have been
> aimed at discrediting the
> very corporation this ship
> serves.

The old man springs to his feet, his hands
slamming on the table in front of him.

> THE OLD MAN
> (spitting words out)
> Who - would - do - such - a
> - thing?

Fire shoots from his eyes as they dance
from man to man.

> THE OLD MAN (CONT'D)
> (angrily)
> Is he here in this room?
> Show him to me!

After a long pause, Bofsky answers.

> BOFSKY
> The only one with the
> authority to sign each of

these direct orders, the
most potent of us, the
supreme power with the
ability to attempt to hide
it all, is *there*.
        (points an accusing hand at the old
        man)
You!

Bofsky strides forward, slamming the data
stick on the table. The old man shrinks
as he plugs the stick in and sees the
irrefutable evidence dance across the
glass. Rapid-fire questions fly around
the room, one OFFICER settling on Bofsky
as the old man is escorted from the room.

                    OFFICER
What else do you know,
OverCapt'n Bofsky? This
information has certainly
come to you over everyone
else. Can you also tell us
the solution we seek to get
this ship back operational?

                    BOFSKY
If the good sers will permit,
I might have a suggestion for
you to try. However, I would
very much like one concession
from this group should my
guess provide the solution to
this catastrophe. I note this
vessel is now without the
services of a captain. My
offer is for an acceptance of
my immediate placement in that
position should my information
be of service to you.

Two high-ranking officers step forward, gesticulating wildly.

                    BOFSKY
          Wait, wait, my good men. I
          know your protests, both of
          you senior to my position
          and due to move up as the
          old man moves out.
          Consider. You have worked
          to resolve this crisis for
          some time. How much
          progress has been made?
          Any? If the solution I have
          been working to effect these
          past units is unsuccessful,
          bump me back to underpriv't.
          What can you lose? The
          alternative is to sit, send
          out an emergency beacon, and
          hope we can survive the
          weeks until help arrives.
          Then we all get bumped back
          to beneath the military
          arm's lowest commissioned
          officer. What can my offer
          hurt?

The others in the room seem to shrink back
where they stand, no one stepping back up
to force Bofsky's hand.

With a smile, Bofsky pulls a second data
stick from his pocket and places it on the
table. Those in the room with Bofsky
glance at it, and then one of the two
high-ranking officers steps up and takes
it.

Bofsky's smile grows wider with his success.

INT. BOFSKY'S PERSONAL QUARTERS - DAY

Bofsky stands in front of a mirror. The ship is operational again, and all lights are on. He stands tall and speaks to himself.

> BOFSKY
> CaptGen'l Willane Bard
> Bofsky, look how far you've come.

Bofsky grins a grin that does not look pleasant at all.

ACT XVI - AFTERMATH

INT. OPERATING ROOM OBSERVATON WINDOW -
DAY (THE PRESENT)

BOFSKY is in front of the observation
window, a look of anticipation on his
face. He holds a NeuroShok stick in his
hand. The observation window is opaque.
Bofsky steps forward, tapping the window.
As it shifts to clarity, blinding
brilliance assaults Bofsky's eyes. Alarm
klaxons start drumming. Bofsky covers his
eyes.

          BOFSKY
      (yelling)
   Are we breached?

A sizzle is heard as the super strong
glassine starts to melt. Fingers of
almost solid brilliance shoot from the far
side of the window into people, painfully
pulling their souls from within, the
people dropping to the floor afterwards.
RJORCK steps through the empty window
frame. He is walking with a strength not
his own, the brilliant fingers of light
streaming from his torso. The fingers of

light shoot from him, reaching through the
doorways.

MONTAGE:

Multiple scenes of the fingers of light
stabbing into people all over the ship are
seen, dropping them lifeless to the floor.
Also seen are the fingers of light
reaching into distant parts of the ship,
taking out souls, twisting equipment and
burning bioware, probing the ship,
searching for Rjorck a way home.

INT.   CORRIDOR - DAY

Rjorck stumbles down a corridor, the light
still flooding from his body. He stands
unsteadily, then steps through a doorway
where he sees a landing pod.

EXT.   BATTLE CRUISER - DAY

The battle cruiser hangs in space above
the beautiful jewel of
Rejuvenant/Se'Yan't. In the blackness of
space, only the two distant suns can be
seen. No stars are visible in the void.
Rjorck's landing pod jettisons from the
battle cruiser. Stabbing fingers of light
are barely contained inside his pod,
seeping from the landing pod. Then, a
massive multi-fingered fist of light
stretches from the pod to the battle
cruiser, burning its way through the hull.

INT.   LANDING POD - DAY

Rjorck stands inside the pod, his arms
spread wide, his feet akimbo, as the last

of his inner well-spring of *poi'ntr'in* power flashes out of him.

MONTAGE:

The brilliance of his *poi'ntr'in* fills the small pod, reaching strong fingers out to the mighty battleship, sliding through melting glassine windows, deep into the ship's weapons systems.

There is a stab on this circuit, a twist of that dial, an overload surge added just so, and the light withdraws.

Rjorck's lifeboat drops him gently through the atmosphere.

Rjorck collapses to the floor of the landing pod.

EXT. LANDING POD - DAY

The landing pod is moving just into the upper atmosphere.

EXT. BATTLE CRUISER - DAY

The battle cruiser hangs in space, black against blacker night, between Se'Yan't's two suns. One sun is half the size of the other. Se'Yan't's yellow atmosphere glows in its brilliance. The battle cruiser shudders. Small ripping explosions of white brilliance sparkle along one panel of the cruiser. Multiple escape pods jettison from the ship, and then in a series of ever-larger flashes of brilliance, the cruiser flashes to a brilliance outshining even the suns on

either side. It shines at full brilliance
a few moments, then fades to nothing as
only the planet and its two suns are left
in the darkness of space.

EXT. ROCKY BEACH - DAY

The landing pod sits on the stones of a
beach. The door to the pod is open.

This is the same beach on which Rjorck
welcomed Adhor'k back from her year in the
sea. Rjorck is collapsed on the stones.

Rjorck is barely breathing, revealing only
the faintest rattling of breath moving in
and out of his lips.

INT. MEGACORP SECURITY DIVISION, EARTH -
DAY

SECURITY OFFICER BRAXTN stands, looking at
information on his 'glass' data monitor.
An emergency message is on the glass over
his desk. He slams his leathery hand down
on the desktop, then reaches out to
manipulate the information on the glass.

> BRAXTN
> Robn't. Get in here!
> (in a harsh voice)
> How the devil did this
> happen? They were just
> there. Now they're not.
> How the *devil* can a star
> cruiser just not *be* there?
> Tell me that, Robn't. How
> the *devil* can they just not
> be there?

Braxtn spins around in his chair and
glares at his subordinate, ROBN'T, then he
snorts.

> BRAXTN (CONT'D)
> My god, it had better not be
> that idiot glitch we had
> last quarter. Tell me that,
> Robn't. Tell me it's not
> that idiot glitch from last
> quarter.
>> (exits room quickly)

> ROBN'T
> S-s-s-sir. I-I-I d-d-don't
> t-t-think s-s-so, Ser.

Robn't reaches in a pocket, pulls out an
information stick, nearly losing it to the
floor as he darts after his commanding
officer, follows the sounds of loud
footsteps, takes shortcuts, and arrives at
Braxtn's office just before Braxtn.

> BRAXTN
> Where the devil have you
> been, Robn't?

Braxtn slams his hand to the glass, the
images flickering at the force, his anger
transmitting into the circuits themselves.

> BRAXTN (CONT'D)
> I've got to have that
> frickin' ship up and
> available. Do you hear me,
> Robn't? Starstrike class
> battleships don't just
> disappear into thin air!

                    ROBN'T
Ser.
        (offers the information stick)
    Ser, this time I think it
    might have done just that.
        (dances away as the stick is whisked
        from his hand)

                    BRAXTN
What the devil does that
mean?

Braxtn thrusts the stick into the terminal
slot, slaps the glass, and mutters to
himself.

                    BRAXTN (CONT'D)
What the devil does this mean?
This can't be right. It's
there. I saw it just minutes
ago. Then, nothing. It was
there, I tell you. Now, look
at this. What is that
signature? An electromagnetic
solar flare? It could be with
those frickin' twin suns. Who
the devil would live on a
planet that near two suns, and
that big one! My god! It
could cook a bird in a
heartbeat. If I owned real
estate there, I'd be out in a
flash, the devil with the
loss. My god, I cannot make
heads nor tails of this.

Braxtn glances up, sees Robn't still
there, and barks.

                    BRAXTN (CONT'D)
I want two teams on this.
Get to PR to get a group
together to contain this
mess. My god! How can a
ship just disappear along
with thousands of people?
There'll be the devil for
somebody to pay, and I'll be
screwed if it'll be me!
          (glares)
I'll be the fool if I'm the
one to pay.

Braxtn chews his jaw, continues his
riveting gaze, and spits out his words.

                    BRAXTN (CONT'D)
Git, you idiot. You think
this is going to fix itself?

                    ROBN'T
          (palatable nervousness)
Ser, what about the second
team you want?

                    BRAXTN
Get it together, man; don't
you have a brain in that
body?

Braxtn spins around, his hand darting to
the glass displaying the unwanted news;
with quick motions, his movements yank
forward new, as yet unseen information.

                    BRAXTN (CONT'D)
There! That! Get a
military team out there to
recover whatever clues are

                    225

           still left. I want
           MegaCorp's best out there
           dropping crap yesterday.
           Nothing can create an
           electromagnetic signature
           that big without some
           evidence left behind. Go
           on, man. Get to work.

Braxtn turns back to the display,
dismissing Robn't with the turn of his
head.

INT.   CONTROL CENTER - DAY

Robn't opens the door into the control
center and steps inside, closing the door
after him. He leans the back of his head
against the wall. The rustle of someone
changing position in the room makes him
look up.

A MAN sits at his desk. The desk is full
of stuff and slightly disorganized.

                MAN AT DESK
           That bad, huh, chief? I'm
           just glad it was your hide
           that got ripped off, and not
           mine. I've been skewered
           too many times by the big
           boss, and I'm glad to let
           you have it anytime.
              (grunt of disgust)

                ROBN'T
           He's up a creek for sure,
           this time. I wouldn't want
           to be him.

Robn't crosses to his desk, his hand waving up the glass as he sits.

> ROBN'T (CONT'D)
> Either we find that ship or he goes down, and you can bet he won't go down alone. Boys, this is a big one. We need to get together two crack teams, one to keep all this under wraps and another to get their butts out there and find out just what the devil happened to that battleship. There must be something out there, residue, floating ion drive traces, organic materials, or *something*.

Robn't taps his glass to bring up the requisition manifests, draws his fingers back from the glass, and sits back, his arms behind his head.

> ROBN'T (CONT'D)
> My bidding.
> (to himself)
> MegaCorp, it's time to do *my* bidding.

INT. CORRIDOR - NIGHT

The lighting is dim, but this ship is a near derelict. A loud rumbling thump is heard, and the ship shudders.

EXT. SHIP - NIGHT

The exterior of the ship is very old and

scarred. A grid of glowing sensors is
placed at frequent intervals. There is a
hole in the side of the ship. Those
sensors just around the hole are
flickering, then the array on half the
ship blinks out.

INT. CAPTAIN'S QUARTERS - NIGHT

Klaxons erupt, and the FREIGHTER TUG
CAPT'N, old, grizzled, and unkempt, jerks
awake.

He stands, unable to catch his breath as
he stumbles to a sensor on the wall.
Lights flash red on the sensor.

               FREIGHTER TUG CAPT'N
Blasters!
   (spittle flies from his lips)
Frickin' meteors! This is
empty space. How could I be
decompressing? Seals
couldn't be gone. I checked
'em back in port.

The captain hits the panel beside the
lights as he closes his eyes, waiting for
the status report to pull up.

               FREIGHTER TUG CAPT'N (CONT'D)
Dang-slow computer.
Probably it doesn't even
know there's a problem, and
I'll die here in my own
vomit.
   (peers from one cracked eyelid)
No, no, no!!! Holed in Bay
E? Good god!

228

INT. CORRIDOR - NIGHT

The captain stumbles down the corridor.
He slaps the control to open an emergency
decompression survival pod. He falls
inside. Air shoots from orifices in the
walls. The captain breathes in deeply,
his eyes clearing. He pulls an emergency
safe-suit from a locker, grabs a breathing
canister, and explores his ship.

Entering Bay E, the captain sees the
damage. A relieved look crawls across his
face when he sees his stash of hooch is
undamaged. However, inside the hold
floats a piece of machinery not on his
cargo manifest. He moves up to inspect
it, finding a fire-damaged label. It
reads:

STARSTRIKE CLASS PROPULSION ACTUATOR ARM
PART 895-4839, ALMARINE MANUFACTURING,
PLUTO STATION.

In smaller letters are seen:

FOR SOLE USE OF MEGACORP CORPORATION. ALL
RIGHTS RESERVED.

The captain pushes it aside to reach to an
emergency panel, pulling out a canister
with the words PATCH-O-TORCH on it. He
also pulls a metal panel from a pile of
materials and starts to seal the hole.

INT. CONTROL ROOM - NIGHT

The captain enters and opens a panel on
the wall, flipping several switches. The
various lights on the panel turn from red

to orange to yellow to green. The air
slowly comes up to standard pressure. At
this, he removes his helmet and puts the
breathing canister aside. He spreads
long-unused charts over the windowless
space. He touches the charts with a
finger, apparently retracing his course.
Pulling out a small reader, he runs it
across the hard copies then plugs it into
a feed line, initiating sensor input.
Seeing the sensor display the realtime
coordinates of the ship's travel
itinerary, he appears perplexed, a frown
on his face, until half of the display
suddenly goes black.

          FREIGHTER TUG CAPT'N
  Not good. Maybe I do have a
  problem.

The captain flips old-fashioned switches
and toggles and groans.

          FREIGHTER TUG CAPT'N (CONT'D)
  Half the mother-scrubbing
  sensors shot to hell. No
  self-triangulation with only
  half the sensor array up.
  This is going to be a long
  trip, maybe even long enough
  for me to find out where I
  am and just what has
  happened.

The captain pulls his reader out, flashing
the image on the wall, running it back to
the collapse of the sensor arrays.

          FREIGHTER TUG CAPT'N (CONT'D)
  There. That is where my

ship went off course.
(absently)
Let me time it back to that
point. I might yet tweak
this computer into telling
me how to get home, even
with using just half the
stars showing in the sky.

The captain spends time at a manual
console, punching in information,
referring to his maps and the information
on the reader, apparently reprogramming
the ship's course. He then moves to
another console with a more modern 'glass'
data display where he composes a message
to MegaCorp, the contents displayed on the
screen. When he is finished, the SEND
prompt comes up prominently displayed.
His hand reaches out with an alcoholic
quiver to approve the command. Then, he
falls to a makeshift bunk in the control
room, and his eyes close. After a minute,
the sound of snoring is heard in the room.

INT. STARGEN'L'S OFFICE - DAY

A shimmering field surrounds STARGEN'L
GRIX'M JANET', indicating a privacy field.
Other people are very vaguely visible in
the background.

                STARGEN'L GRIX'M JANET'
That's what no one can
understand, ser. This *is*
starstrike class. No, no
one knew about the mission,
ser. It was certainly kept
under the tightest of wraps.
Yes, ser, I know what this

could mean to the
corporation if word leaked
out that one of our ships
was in the vicinity of
Rejuvenant when we lost
contact with it. Thank you,
ser. I will, ser.

Janet' breaks the connection, and the
privacy field fades. A large conference
room peopled with real people and holo
representatives sharpens into focus. A
large glassine clearwall fills the
background with the city seen just beyond.
Janet' looks around growling, his aide
BEN'FRN at his side.

> STARGEN'L GRIX'M JANET'
> (CONT'D)
Who's seen this report from
that freighter out in the
arm?

An arm or realistic facsimile from every
attendee begrudges acknowledgement.

> STARGEN'L GRIX'M JANET'
> (CONT'D)
Ben'frn, have we contacted
the capt'n, yet? Do we know
anything more than just what
he sent us in that slo-trak?

Janet' sees the nervous eyes flicking back
and forth at each other, and he slams his
fist on the real-wood table, lashing out.

> STARGEN'L GRIX'M JANET'
> (CONT'D)
Then find something out!

(several proxy holos flicker, while
flesh copies jerk)
Our military arm is known
for supporting the policies
of GlobalPresident Benetin.
Our other activities are
entirely secretive. Each of
you knows that. To update
each of you on this mission,
CaptGen'l Willane Bofsky was
given unprecedented liberty
to achieve the required
objective no matter what the
cost. As of the last
received transmission, he
had been rather permissive
in allowing his crew to
attempt to persuade the
inhabitants of Rejuvenant to
accommodate our requests for
certain information they
possessed. It would seem
this information was unable
be acquired even at the cost
of the indigenous
intelligent life found on
the planet.
(pauses and looks around)
Here is one of our major
concerns in this situation.
Rejuvenant was known to be
an unarmed planet. Yet, our
most advanced starstrike
battleship cruiser simply
winked out within one AU of
the suns of the Rejuvenant
system. My best analysts
say it was even closer,
perhaps within a quarter
light year. There was no

warning that we have been made aware of. There have been no reports received from any nearby quarters indicating any unusual activity in the area, and at this point, sers, we are, without question, clueless. Does anyone have any input or suggestions in this matter?

                    BRN' FRN
Um, ser, could this possibly be something new?

                    STARGEN'L GRIX'M JANET'
Be specific, man! Something new like what?

                    BEN' FRN
Ser, a new class of technology or even a new race of sentient beings?

                    STARGEN'L GRIX'M JANET'
Am I always to be surrounded by idiots? A new race of sentient beings? May God save us from the idiots at our sides! Out! Out! All of you, out!

Janet' presses the heels of his hands to his forehead, shaking his head back and forth until the room is emptied, proxy holos blinking out and flesh forms scurrying out the door.

The stargen'l touches a sensor on the

table in front of him. The static and
clatter of a message explodes into the
room, the alcoholic tremor in the voice
clear.

FREIGHTER TUG CAPT'N
This is the capt'n of the
freighter-tug, Capps'nian,
out of Wendy's World. I
have a piece of one of your
ships you might be
interested in, a starstrike
class propulsion actuator
arm. It might go cash to
the highest buyer. Are any
of you in there interested?

STARGEN'L GRIX'M JANET'
My god, what a note to end
on, and him still years
away.

Janet' walks to the clearwall and looks
out over the city spread out before him.
His shoulders begin to sag as he stands
there.

ACT XVII - BACKLASH

INT.   MEGACORP BOARDROOM - DAY

STARGEN'L GRIX'M JANET' wears formal
civilian ceremonial robes. He grimaces
then straightens as he steps in the
MegaCorp boardroom seen earlier.

>   STARGEN'L GRIX'M JANET'
> Gentle Sers, let me acquaint
> you with some matters that
> in the past have not been
> deemed worthy of your
> concern. One of these
> matters is the true nature
> of the so-called defensive
> capabilities of our company
> battle cruisers. Recently
> one of our most state-of-
> the-art starstrike class
> cruisers was sent to an
> isolated system of two
> tidally locked stars. You
> may have heard of the
> inhabited planet that
> revolves around one of these
> stars. It is the garden
> planet Rejuvenant. Over the

years, information has been
collected to very strongly
suggest the indigenous
peoples had developed a
process for the indefinite
extension of life. In an
effort to obtain this
process, our cruiser was
sent out to negotiate with
the inhabitants of this
planet. It would seem that
the negotiations got a
little one-sided, and as of
the last registered report
received, the local populace
had succumbed to the
capt'n's interrogation
methods.

(looks around the boardroom)
It is unknown just how, but
we have lost contact with
the cruiser. It would seem
to have simply vanished
except for one isolated
message received from an old
freighter-tug plying the
area at sub-light speed. It
claims to have been damaged
by a fragment of the before-
mentioned cruiser, retaining
the fragment in a damaged
hold.

(pauses)
As you might imagine, plans
to contain the financial and
political fallout have been
initiated . . .

(uproar from the men at the table;
speaks to himself)
And that's the good

news . . .

Janet' steps back, peering around the
room, as further pandemonium continues to
erupt around the room.

INT.   WORLDPRESIDENTIAL CORRESPONDENCE
CHAMBERS - DAY

A TEAM OF MEN AND WOMEN each sit at a
computer 'glass' at his or her
workstation.   This is a room where
information flows into and out of the
worldpresident's ears.   One of the team
members is reading information on a
'glass' and calls out to the rest.

                1st VOICE
    Hey, look what just came in.
    Let me get this up on the
    wall.
        (loudly)
    Hey! You want to see this!

The team member manipulates something on
the glass, and the same image rolls onto
the wall sized 'glass' for everyone to
see.   The men and women gather in groups,
regather, and seem flustered.   The message
they see is as follows:

*TRANSMISSION 16/000873862.45682
VERIFIED.   SECURITY LEVEL
ALPHA.PROXY.DOG.   ORIGIN OF
TRANSMISSION: BAR'AKKER'ENT
WORLD.   RECEIPIENT:
GLOBALPRESIDENT BENETIN.
IMMEDIATE REPLY TRANSMISSION
URGENTLY REQUESTED.   Official*

*government use only. Violaters
will be prosecuted to the fullest
extent of the law.
Interplanetary Code 4418.164003.*

*My Most Humble Greetings to
GlobalPresident Benetin. In this
time of interplanetary peace and
prosperity, it is most vital to
maintain the open lines of
communication that enable our vast
multi-global civilization to survive
the calamities that history has
shown to be most detrimental to
single planet cultures. With that
in mind, rumors of the utmost
concern have reached my ears.*

*As per our most recent meeting at
the Glok'dik Trans-Planet
conference, financial prosperity is
agreed to be paramount to the
survival of the social ties binding
the many planets of our
civilization. One of the most
stable financial institutions in the
entire worlds we know is based on
your homeworld of Earth. This
institution is, of course, the
corporation known by both name and
logo as MegaCorp or MC. While
widely noted as the most
unprecedented and recognizable name
throughout all the known worlds, and
while the good MC does cannot be
disputed, a concern has arisen.*

*As recently as two local planetary
cycles ago, reports were circulating*

239

regarding the aggressive nature of MC's advances toward my homeworld, Rejuvenant. Your records will show my previous query regarding this matter as little as one-quarter local planetary cycle ago (TRANSMISSION 16/000873862.42093.09). I understand that proof of misdeeds must be the basis of accusations, and without these proofs, action on a matter can be very difficult to initiate.

I believe action must now be initiated. Your office has affirmed by its very charter the sanctity of human life and the due diligence private enterprise must pursue in the respect of that sanctity. That very diligence has now been so severely abused as to be nonexistent.

All communication from my homeworld, Rejuvenant, has ceased. Any and all attempts to contact Rejuvenant have been futile. In the local planetary cycle preceding this unprecedented collapse of communication between my homeworld and myself, numerous messages of concern were transmitted directly to my domicile via sublight slow-link concerning the aggressive advances of MC. The transmitter was a person of some note on Earth, the Munificent Rjorck of longstanding repute on your planet. This Rjorck was, as I am, also a native of Rejuvenant. His concerns were my

concerns. While I encouraged him to
absent himself from Rejuvenant until
this pending crisis resolved itself,
his concern for the homeworld
overpowered my entreaties for
caution. Since returning to warn my
peoples, it is feared this Rjorck
has been silenced for his views
concerning MC's aggressive stance
toward Rejuvenant.

While caution is always a wise
stance when extreme measures are to
be considered, I fear that caution
in this situation is a measure we
cannot afford ourselves. I fear
great harm may have already befallen
my fellow citizens of Rejuvenant.
If you can find it in yourself to
take great strides toward pursuing
the resolution of this difficulty,
my greatest gratitude will certainly
put myself in your debt.

Your honorable and extreme
supporter,
GrandSet ComChair Ren'xe t'Le
Frieks'n, Rstt.con.WorldBrittain.ene
WORLD CITIZEN OF REJUVENANT, LOCAL
NAME OF SE'YAN'T
CURRENT POSTING: BAR'AKKER'ENT WORLD
END TRANSMISSION. VERIFICATION CODE
GBERY847DI73.

The message scrolls past on the wall
'glass' with several of the team members
enlarging certain interesting parts,
reading it aloud. Much of it is not read
aloud, though.

                    2nd VOICE
Shall we tell him?

                    3rd VOICE
Let's think through this
carefully. Here we have a
clear accusation of
malfeasance by MegaCorp.
Now, what does that mean to
us here on Earth? Of all
the inhabited worlds, our
planet is one of the oldest
socially and economically.
We are long established, and
what Earth does carries a
great deal of clout with the
newer governments found
elsewhere. Over the years,
our economy has had its ups
and downs. It has been very
strong for years due to the
overwhelming strength and
power of one and only one
corporation. This
corporation has made itself
known as a power throughout
all the known worlds, both
economically and militarily.
Do we really think all the
successes MegaCorp provides
for Earth come with no
price? Just as long as the
price paid is far, far away,
what is that to us? I say
to let sleeping dogs lie.
Just as the transmission
states, there is no proof.
What is one person who
chooses not to be found? He
is of no concern to us.

                    242

                    4th VOICE
You do realize we cannot
really hide this direct
request. It will make it to
Benetin eventually.

                    3rd VOICE
Eventually is not today.
Let matters take their
course. Let it alone long
enough, and it may even fade
into the background. I say
to let it go. Agreed?

                    5th VOICE
While this transmission
might be a little higher
placed, it's similar to the
others we've kept back about
this same thing. None of
those have proven a problem.
I agree. Let it go.
        (voices of agreement)

INT.   LORITMAR OBSERVATORY - NIGHT

A long-established astronomer, DR.SCI.
REFREN ASCOTT, sits at a desk. The room
looks much as any well-funded astronomical
outpost would appear. Behind the
astronomer is a bank of scientific
instruments displaying readouts. Dr.Sci.
Refren Ascott is looking at a display
glass on his desk.

                    DR.SCI. REFREN ASCOTT
Run that report one more
time. This just doesn't
look right.

                    243

>   (stands, strides to main interface
>   bank)
>   Do you have it, yet? I need
>   that information up now so I
>   can balance the patterns in
>   the memory log of this
>   week's reports. For some
>   reason, we've picked up some
>   really odd EMP readings.
>   (watches the report being downloaded
>   into a portable glass)
>   Have any other sectors
>   reported this anomaly? The
>   EMP output is certainly a
>   cause for alarm. I see no
>   way this could be a natural
>   occurrence.

Ascott reaches over to pick up the 'glass'
as the technician shakes her head no. He
walks away with it, studying the
information, finally winding up at the
base to a very massive, very old, yet very
well-maintained telescope. Ascott uses
one hand to manipulate unseen information
on the portable 'glass.'

The portable glass' display shows Ascott's
report on top with an internal news feed
running beneath it. As the words
STARSTRIKE CLASS BATTLESHIP GOES MISSING
IN THE VICINITY OF A DISTANT DUAL STAR
SYSTEM scroll by, Ascott's hand pushes his
report to the back and pulls the news
report to the top.

>   ASCOTT
>   (to himself)
>   Hmm. This is certainly not
>   news for the general public.

                    Only MegaCorp has starstrike
                    class. They must be really
                    sitting on this one.
                         (tapping glass, thinking)
                    That *could* produce a high
                    enough EMP to create those
                    readings we picked up.
                         (pause)
                    The location of this station
                    might be key.

Ascott pauses again, then he voices his
opinion absently.

                    ASCOTT (CONT'D)
                    I wouldn't be surprised if
                    this spot we're at happens
                    to be as near to that binary
                    system as any other
                    civilized outpost.

Ascott looks back to the technician.

                    ASCOTT (CONT'D)
                    Just where is that dual star system?

Ascott continues to interact with the
technician, and the scene dims as the
headlines from the next montage overlay on
top of the two men's images. Ascott and
the technician continue to work as the
headlines appear and fade away.

MONTAGE:

INT. SERIES OF NEWS FEED HEADLINES - DAY

We see these flash across layered on top
of each other. Each sinks, expands, and
fades as a new one is introduced.

MARCH 1.   NEWSTRIBUNE.   NEW YORK, EARTH.
UNPRECEDENTED DISCOVERY BY PROMINENT
ASTRONOMER

MARCH 3.   INTERGALACTICNEWS.NEWS.   ARES
CITY, MARS.   MEGACORP STUMBLES

MARCH 11.   SAN FRANCISCO EXAMINER.   NEW
SAN FRANCISCO, EARTH.   THE BATTLESHIP – IS
NO NEWS REALLY GOOD NEWS?

APRIL 17.   WORLD GEOGRAPHIC.   EARTH.
CRACK SEEN IN MEGACORP'S FAÇADE

INT.   CITYGVN'R'S OFFICE – NIGHT

CITYGVN'R REENSON walks across a very
large and elegant office.   An elegant desk
is unadorned except for one brown
envelope.   Reenson picks it up, looking
over it as if mystified as to its
construction or purpose.

Reenson smells it and strokes it.   Her
puzzled expression suddenly changes to
laughter as she comments to herself.

            REENSON
    Paper!   I should have
    remembered that!

With difficulty, Reenson works the
envelope open, mumbling.

            REENSON (CONT'D)
    Texting for the poor, that's
    all paper is.

She immediately glances around, although

it is clear she is alone; she seems embarrassed at the comment.

Reenson unfolds a sheaf of papers from inside the envelope, leafing through them as if unsure just how to work with words on paper. She turns one page upside down, then turns it back the way it was. She glances at the back of each sheet, and then holds them under a light to brighten them up. Finally she goes to a leather chair by the real wood fireplace that is burning merrily, turns a lamp on, and sits.

INTERCUT SCENES AS FOLLOWS:

Reenson reads the letter aloud. The scene goes back and forth between the live action she reads about in the letter and Reenson physically reading the words. Sometimes, one is overlaid on the other with Reenson's words as a voice over.

Dear CityGvn'r,

We don't got much here down in the city, not much that ain't been thrown away by one of you. One thing we got is our pride, though. We are born and die, just like you, and when things go good, life is happy for us. Sometimes things ain't so good, though. Lots of us just barely get by. Getting food is hard, and getting sick is likely a death sentence. But we do what we can, and sometimes life is good.
Now, MegaCorp, there. They been good to us. Wherever we go, they

sell us stuff. We can get it at
fair prices. My wife, she worked in
a MegaSales center for a long time.
She didn't make much, but they was
good to her, and she liked her work.
She got real sick there for a while,
and we all understood she had to be
let go. You can't keep paying
someone and have to hire someone
else to do their job. But it was
tough when she was let go. They did
throw her a nice little party when
she left, and gave her a little cake
and all. She did enjoy that. She
kept the little decorations until
the day she died, kept 'em by her
bedside and all. She always thought
of MegaCorp as a guarding angel.

But now, we're all together. We
don't think MegaCorp's on our side
anymore. Sure, when times got
really tough, the money from sending
our boys and girls to the academy
was a godsend. Lots of us used that
money for feeding our families,
otherwise we wouldn't have had
anything to eat. We appreciated it.
We really did. But now things seem
different.

That ship they say went down out
there in space. All those kids were
on board. MegaCorp won't tell us
nothing. Myself, I got a nephew on
board. Never had kids of my own,
the wife getting sick and all. But
that boy I thought of as my own.
He's only twenty turns old. He
should be fighting for us, for our
betterment, for the good of MegaCorp
and all us down here in the city.

*Now he's just dead from what they
say. Gone. And they don't tell us
nothing.*

*Me and all the people I know feel
the need to do something. Well,
they won't listen to us talk, so we
feel there might be more than one
way to talk. We've got some stuff
stored up, all of us do. A couple
of us have little pieces of ground
we can grow things in. Our clothes
will last us a few more turns. We
think we don't need to buy from
MegaCorp anymore. A few of us still
have jobs there. We can sure take
their money, but that don't mean
they'll get any more of ours.*

*This might not make much of a
difference. But if enough of us got
together, maybe they'd have to
listen. That's why we're writing
you. We don't have much skills at
these kinds of things. We just
figured if enough of us signed this
petition, you might be willing to
get something going, talk with some
other high-placed folk, get the ball
rolling, just do what you got to do.*

*Please help us. We can't do this
on our own. We don't know how.*

> *Yours,*
> *Johnie L. Bean*

Reenson holds the letter as her hand drops
to the arm of the chair. She looks into
the fire as she shakes her head. She
picks up the papers and flips through the
dozens of pages attached, yet to be read.

                    REENSON
My god. All these names.
No telling how long it took
to go from person to person
gathering all these names.
This is the story that'll
get the ball going against
that monstrosity. I
couldn't have put together
anything better if I'd
assembled a team of public
relations nerds to work on
this for two weeks. I won't
even need to rewrite this.
They treat his sick wife
like dirt, and she grovels
for them. They take their
children for a few dollars.
These poor people. How can
I not give them all the help
I can?

Reenson reaches beside her chair for a
portable 'glass,' and she strokes its
surface, awakening the transmitting
circuits inside. With the spare movements
born of much practice, she gently pushes
and tugs the information within.

                    REENSON
        (with satisfaction)
Evey high level contact I
know needs this, and it's
now on its way.

Reenson stands and takes the letter to her
desk. She opens a drawer and her personal
safe inside, placing the letter safely
within its confines.

INT.   VOTING ASSEMBLY FLOOR - DAY

This is a political assembly voting floor.
This is an old-fashioned room with richly
adorned buttress held in place by carved
cherubim. Chimes go off, and red lights
blink, green taking their place. Numerous
amber lights indicate abeyances. There is
a low hum of activity over all the events.
There is a lag as votes are tallied by
hand. A crash of a wooden mallet sounds
as the giant display overhead displays the
results of the voting process. Everyone,
no matter how they voted, stands and
cheers, as if the victory is indeed
theirs.

Far above in the upstairs observation
room, the real-glass windows silence the
sounds of the voting floor. The
WORLDGOV'R stands inside the room, where
the mood is more reserved.

                 WORLDGOV'R
     An old-fashioned process for
     an old-fashioned system.

The worldgov'r laughs indulgently, looking
at REENSON. He waits for a moment as the
results are displayed.

                 WORLDGOV'R (CONT'D)
     Well, what about that!
     MegaCorp to be dismembered.
     I wouldn't count on this
     making any real difference,
     you know.
          (swirls a frothy liquid around in
          his glass)
     Sure, they've voted to slap

MegaCorp's wrist, but that's
all it will be. A slap.
Sure, they've phrased their
vote to appeal to the little
guy, but the little guy
wouldn't know the difference
between a $40K fine and a
$40B fine. All the numbers
are just that, big numbers.

He sips from his glass, his tongue holding
the froth at bay while the bitter liquid
burns down his throat.

                REENSON
I should know that.
    (sighs)
I wish I could say that the
people who started all this
would see something from it,
but the types of changes
they need are beyond
anything I can do.
    (looks out over the floor, the
    tinted real-glass hiding her
    observations)
There they are, putting on a
show for the people they
claim to represent. At
least we got this, however
small a victory it might be.
God knows the corporation
will simply sic some World-
lawyers on this, dumbing
down the effects until they
mean nothing at all. If
MegaCorp wasn't the glue
holding Earth's economy
together, I'd sure like to
stick it to them. For the

little guy.
                    WORLDGOV'R
We'll see that your little
guys get something. At
least the ones who signed
that petition. We'll show
them taking a chance like
that has its rewards. And
remember.
          (pauses, walking over to the window
          to stand beside the citygvn'r)
Those guys down there still
get to vote on the
sentencing. This might still
get really good after all.

The worldgov'r throws his head back,
taking the last of the bitter liquor and
its sickeningly sweet foam into his mouth.

INT. MEGACORP HEADQUARTERS - DAY

A VERIFICATION TEAM is on an inspection of
the MegaCorp headquarters building to
ensure it has been vacated and is no
longer operational. Enormous hallways,
huge office suites, and finally the main
boardroom greet them. All the glassine
walls are opaque, but the iconic symbol
above the great table, though no longer
operational, tells them for sure where
they are.

                    1st TEAM MEMBER
Hey. Look at this.
          (all turn to look up)
I saw this on the Vid once.
I never thought I'd see it
in person, though.

2nd TEAM MEMBER
Yeah. They sure shackled
the beast, didn't they?

INT. COURT ROOM - DAY

The ruling elite of MegaCorp are all
assembled here.

GLOBALPRESIDENT BENETIN
Revenge is such an ugly
word.
(glares at MegaCorp officers)
What you have done with your
company in the name of
profit has been heinous.
Entire worlds have suffered
for your gain. If you
couldn't buy people out at
fire-sale prices, your
military arm cleared them
out with weapons and
firepower.

Benetin walks across the chamber in front
of the convicted officers, his gaze
riveting each one in turn.

GLOBALPRESIDENT BENETIN
(CONT'D)
Not only did you take what
you wanted in the way of
resources, you took from
people who had no choice but
to depend on your for their
very substance, your
employees. You drove them
into the ground, paid them a
pauper's wage, and washed
your hands of them as soon

as they were no longer of
use to you. But the most
heinous act of all was the
buying of children in order
to indoctrinate them into
your military arm, owned
lock, stock, and barrel by
MegaCorp. They were nothing
more than slaves to your
corporation. Each of you
disgusts me. Several of you
have claimed plausible
deniability. Let that fly
in an appellate court of
law. You may feel the
harshness of this sentence
is more than enough, but
rest assured, you should
feel very lucky that your
only penalties have been to
be banned from ownership in
any MegaCorp-owned or
controlled company and
banishment from Earth for a
minimum of ten standard
years.
    (pausing)
Be grateful. If my input
had been heeded, you would
not have gotten off so
lightly.

Benetin dismisses the scum without another
look, his quick steps carrying him out of
the hall.

                MAGISTRATE
        Sers, you have heard from
        the highest political power
        on this planet. I must

concur with each point he
has made. Consider
yourselves fortunate. At
this time you will be
escorted to a waiting
transport for immediate
deportation. A limited line
of credit has been
established for you, good
for one local year on the
planet of your destination.
At the end of that time
period, you must have made
arrangements to provide for
yourself as no additional
funds will be made
available, and any funds
still unaccessed will be
rescinded from your control.
Use these funds well, sers.

The magistrate turns and begins addressing
the team overseeing the transition of
MegaCorp into two separate entities,
military and economic.

MAGISTRATE (CONT'D)
Sers, it is imperative that
teams be sent immediately at
MegaCorp's expense to
explore the areas of the
reported anomalies that
started this entire affair.
I understand there was an
altercation leaving
Rejuvenant's population
decimated. I expect to see
ongoing reports transmitted
directly to me summarizing
the results of the teams,

and that is plural with an s, sers, because I mean teams sent to survey the damage on Rejuvenant. I hope to hear that there were survivors on that world. If not, I expect to see that the resources and infrastructure are thoroughly surveyed with the intent of allocating these items to the remaining off-world populace. Of course, in any case, there may be those who wish to return to their homeworld. This desire must be accommodated, whatever that entails. This mission is entrusted to make sure any necessary repairs, restoration, or construction is immediately initiated to ensure that no one with a legal claim to that planet is denied his or her wishes in returning as soon as humanly possible. This court will pursue answers and retribution if it even suspects this directive is not being given one hundred percent compliance, no matter the cost to MegaCorp Corporation. Both the economic and military arms may be called upon to effectively wrap up this directive in a timely manner. Am I clearly understood?

Without even a chance for the transition
team to formulate a reply, the magistrate
leaves the hall, his anger still
resounding from the walls. The transition
team, relieved to be out of his presence,
looks for the quickest way to the exit.

ACT XVIII - RECOVERY BEGINS

EXT. RIVERBANK - DAY

BRAXTN stands in casual fishing clothes on
a river bordered by dry dirt and patchy
grass. High cliffs erupt on the far side
of the river. Braxtn seems more
weathered, as if perhaps he is tired of
fighting. A VISITOR in corporate attire
is at his side. The man hands Braxtn a
'glass' unit. Braxtn takes it
reluctantly.

                    BRAXTN
                (growling)
            Get the devil out of my
            face, boy!

Braxtn kicks dirt, showering his visitor;
when the man continues to stand there,
Braxtn slams his fishing gear and the
glass he has been given to his feet.

                    BRAXTN (CONT'D)
            Curse you and your
            corporation! You knew I
            couldn't turn this down.
            How dare you bait me back

into MegaCorp! You dirt
bag. I'll do this for you.
Yeah, I'll be there to lead
your team. But the devil
take you if this doesn't
give me back my good name.
MegaCorp *stole* that from me.
> (picks up the 'glass' from his feet,
> now cracked)

                VISITOR
We can get you a new one of
those, ser.

                BRAXTN
Blast it, boy. Does it
still work?

Braxtn brushes the dirt off and sees the
image flickering from the damage.

Braxtn's hand begins pulling up
information, manipulating it with twists
and turns of his fingers that never quite
touch the glass, already back at work,
already back in the element he has so
missed the past half year.

The visitor smiles at him. As the visitor
turns and walks away, he grins broadly,
holding a small instrument to his mouth,
and he speaks into it.

                VISITOR
Thank your lucky ladies,
Ser. Braxtn's back on
board. I don't know who the
idiot was who let him get
away in the first place.

EXT.   SNOW-COVERED STREET - DAY

It is snowing heavily. A WOMAN is wearing
a luxuriant fur-collared coat. She pulls
her furred collar closer. She crumples an
unopened sheaf of paper into her pocket.
Tears run down her face. With one hand
she brushes the moisture from her face.

INT.   WOMAN'S DWELLING - DAY

          WOMAN
     (tears falling down her face)
     Paper! Am I that poor, now?
     (sobs)
     They're right. I don't even
     own a glass anymore. All I
     have is my coat.
        (reaches to stroke the collar)

She fumbles, unsure how to get inside the
paper. When she finally does, she slips
the contents out. Two smaller papers fall
to the floor as she unfolds the largest.
The word MegaCorp and the MegaCorp logo
are easily seen. She drops the paper and
collapses.

          WOMAN
     MegaCorp! Haven't they
     abused me enough?
        (sobs)

INT.   BEDROOM - NIGHT

The noise of an incoming message breaks
the quiet. A woman, SUNSETT, sits up in
bed. She shakes the man, ENS'T, next to
her.

                    ENS'T
What is it?

                    SUNSETT
Ens't, wake up. You've got
a call.

                    ENS'T
                 (slurred)
Baby, you could have gotten
that and let me sleep.

Ens't sits up, his feet jerking back from
the cold floor, and he stumbles into the
next room. He opens the call.

                ENS'T (CONT'D)
Ens't here. Can't you check
the time? It's . . .

Ens't pauses, grabbing his 'glass,' and
taps the time to the front.

                ENS'T (CONT'D)
. . . two in the morning.

Ens't gives an audible groan and throws
himself onto a padded bench.

                    VOICE
            (crackling, full of static)
Trust me, buddy. You want
to take this call.
            (peal of static-laced laughter)
You really do want to take
this call. You know that
bombshell that nearly took
out MegaCorp? I've got us
on the gravy train to help

clean up the mess. Get your
lazy butt out of Sunsett's
bed and get the hell on a
transport out here. I've
got a message stick on the
way to you encoded with all
the details, that and a nice
chunk of change. This is
the opportunity we've been
looking for. By the way,
it's five-thirty in the
evening out here in the real
world, you pile of crap.
See you in two weeks.

Ens't groans again as the line goes dead.

EXT. SNOW-COVERED STREET - DAY

This time the woman is outside in the snow
without her coat. She is ecstatic. She
is holding the paper as if it is gold.
She hugs herself. A glimpse of the
paper's message as she reads parts of it
aloud tell why.

*MEGACORP CORPORATION IS FULLY FUNDING AN
EXPLORATORY TEAM TO INVESTIGATE THE
ANOMALY RECENTLY DISCOVERED BY DR.SCI.
REFREN ASCOTT OF THE LORITMAR OBSERVATORY
AND THE ANOMALY'S EFFECTS ON THE PLANET
REJUVENANT. YOU ARE HEREBY INVITED TO
JOIN OUR TEAM AS AN HONORED PARTICIPANT.
YOUR EXPERTISE WILL BE FULLY REMUNERATED
IN APPRECIATION FOR YOUR SERVICE AND
COOPERATION. PLEASE SEND ONLY REGRETS.
YOU ACCEPTANCE MAY BE ACKNOWLEDGED BY YOUR
ATTENDANCE AT THE ORGANIZATIONAL MEETING
SCHEDULED AS STATED ON THE FOLLOWING PAGE.
WE HOPE TO SEE YOU THERE. ALL TRAVEL*

EXPENSES WILL BE ADVANCED DIRECTLY TO YOU.
USE TRAVEL CODE 34.LKJ987.45.

> WOMAN
> They need me back! I'm
> going back!

EXT. SPACEPORT LOADING DOCK - DAY

A DOCKWORKER is directing loading crews
for the flotilla to Rejuvenant/Se'Yan't.
She is loudly telling someone something
cannot go in the hold and will be fine on
one of the military transports. Shortly,
someone runs out to deliver her a portable
'glass.'

On the glass is this message:

REGISTRY OF INTERNAL DOCKING AND LOADING
PRIORITIES. PREMIER IMPORTANCE. It has
been noted that certain shipments for the
survey and reconstruction teams to
Rejuvenant have been rerouted to military
transport. This is not to be continued.
Only authorized personnel will receive
permissions to modify cargo manifests and
loading procedures. Anyone receiving a
request to do so should immediately
request verification of authorizations.
Full documentation of the change and the
individual initiating the change must be
duly noted on the manifest. Thank you.

The woman cuts her eyes up to an
observation platform far above as she
stuffs the glass onto a shelf behind her.
She turns and smirks.

                    DOCKWORKER
                (viciously)
            It's my floor. Let's see
            you tell me what I can and
            cannot do. I'll get it done
            my way. Just you see.

INT. SPACEPORT LOADING FLOOR - DAY

Many people are going about their
business. All are wearing earpieces for
communication in the noise. Suddenly,
they all duck, hands grabbing ear-mounted
commlinks in pain as a voice speaks.

                    ENS'T
                (loudly ringing with feedback)
            Has anyone seen that lazy
            idiot, Ollen?

Ens't waits a moment and puts down a comm
headset attached to a master sending unit.
He shrugs his shoulders.

                    ENS'T
            Well, it didn't hurt to ask.
            I can just go look where all
            the women are.

Ens't walks off jauntily through the
workers, whistling, his hands in his
pockets.

INT. SECURITY OFFICE - DAY

BRAXTN is looking at reports on his glass.
A number of names, all with green checks
after them, scroll past. Two appear with
red X's.

                    BRAXTN
        (tapping com button)
    Offc'r, get in here.
        (turning to officer)
    Two of these men. I need to
    know who hired them on.
    Ollen and Ens't. I know
    these men personally. Good
    at their jobs when they
    choose to do them. *If* they
    choose to do them. Good at
    the women, too. That'll be
    the real rub. We don't need
    silly dalliances screwing
    around with this team's
    cohesion. Better yet, get
    them both in here today. I
    want this cleared up before
    we get any further along
    this path of action. Thank
    you. That's all. You may
    go.
            (watches the man leave, gives a nod
            of satisfaction)

LATER THAT DAY:

Braxtn is angry. He is standing behind a
desk. OLLEN and ENS'T are across the desk
from him. They are standing side by side.
Both men are rather seedy looking.

                    BRAXTN
    Lipstick? That's lipstick
    on your face? My god,
    that's why you were kicked
    out of MegaCorp's services
    in the first place. Tell me
    this. Was the girl a member
    of either the survey or

                    266

reconstruction teams? And
the answer had better be no,
because we can't afford to
start selections all over
again.
          (pauses with no response)
I'm taking that for a no.
Men, you'd better keep those
wicks dry while you're on my
watch, or you might not have
any wicks to play your games
with. Is that clearly
understood?
          (slaps his open hand on his desktop)
Men?
          (Ollen and Ens't finally jump, nod,
          and exit rapidly)

EXT. SPACEPORT LOADING DOCK - NIGHT

The dockworker from the earlier scene is
not happy. Several people are arguing
with her. She glances up to see that the
observation deck is conveniently dark.

                    DOCKWORKER
I don't care what the
freakin' paperwork says. I
run this loading facility,
and those containers go
where I say they go. Now
get your butts on the ball
before I crush *your* balls.

She glances back at the darkened
observation platform and grins.

INT. SHIP'S LOUNGE - EVENING

A tall, stemmed glass half filled with a

golden liquid is moving in a circular
pattern, the liquid inside swirling.

Carefully manicured fingers tilt the glass
to sensuous lips. A woman is arm-in-arm,
walking with a man, a clearwall of
glassine showing the blackness of space
and other ships in the flotilla already en
route to Rejuvenant/Se'Yan't. In the
background are other people in dressy
evening clothes, none expensive, sitting
and enjoying the lounge of a mighty
MegaCorp transport ship.

INT. SLOW-SLEEP BAYS - NIGHT

Braxtn is patrolling through the slow-
sleep bays, the bunks sealed for the trip.
Most team members are traveling in this
style, and the bays stretch out before
Braxtn. At each bunk, Braxtn pauses and
peers inside. From time to time, he makes
comments.

> BRAXTN
> My god, was I ever that
> young?
> > (at another bunk)
> I have been old too long.
> > (yet later)
> They are all so beautiful.

Braxtn pauses at one bunk. He wipes the
condensation from the glassine and leans
his forehead onto its surface. He
breathes deeply and closes his eyes.

FLASHBACK/DREAM SEQUENCE:

EXT. OUTDOOR GATHERING - DAY

Braxtn is outside. This memory looks soft
and a bit hazy as if from very long ago.
A woman, TIANNE, is busy at something.

                    BRAXTN
        Tianne! Tianne, you're
        alive again!

Braxtn runs to her. He is also young and
smooth skinned.

                    TIANNE
            (runs her hand along his face)
        Of course I am, dear Brax.
        Why do you say 'again'? You
        old silly, you. I never
        know what will come out of
        your mouth each time I see
        you. I do love you so.

Tianne cups her hand around his neck,
kissing him.

                    BRAXTN
        I'm an old man now, Tianne.
        You should see me. MegaCorp
        has been shattered, and I've
        been given a second chance.
        You would be proud of what
        I'm doing now.

Braxtn watches her, puzzled when he
realizes she is laughing.

                    TIANNE
        Why, you're not hearing a
        single word I'm saying, you
        mean beast. Look at you,
        that hound-dog look on your

face. What is all this
about a second chance? And
you an old man? What does
that make me? Twenty-four?
Why, you mean man, I don't
want to be twenty-four for
another three years. Let's
go somewhere, Brax. I have
missed you so.

Holding her arm, Braxtn follows her.
Leaning in close, he closes his eyes and
breathes deep of her hair.

BACK TO SLOW-SLEEP BAYS:

Braxtn starts, rubbing his cold forehead.
He steps back. Braxtn sees his reflection
in the glassine.

FLASHBACK:

Braxton's unlined face laughs and smiles
as Tianne's hand brushes his cheek.

BACK TO SLOW-SLEEP BAYS:

Braxtn's reflection refocuses to show
Braxtn's reflection as the old man he is.
He looks again at the girl inside the
slow-sleep bunk, and he notices that,
while pretty, she doesn't look so very
much like his Tianne after all.

          BRAXTN
My Tianne. You were never
here. Never at all.
     (pause)
And I am no longer the young
man I once was.

270

Braxtn's eyes tear up and his lip quivers.
Then, he visibly gathers control, and he
begins to move down through the bay,
stopping at every bunk to check on the
occupant inside.

INT. CARGO BAY - DAY

The sweat-stained face of a CARGO HANDLER
twists into disgust.

                CARGO HANDLER
        For crying out loud, will
        you look in this crate?
            (slaps the manifest in his glass)
        This is the third crate in
        just this hold. What idiot
        loaded this bird?

The cargo handler holds onto portable
steps as his workmate climbs up for
verification of the disaster.

                CARGO HANDLER (CONT'D)
        Ti'nene, do you have any
        inkling how hard your next
        few weeks are going to be?
        You might as well cancel all
        those call girls you have
        lined up. They won't be
        getting any. Not from you
        at any rate. Let's pack it
        up for this workday. We'll
        tear these crates apart
        tomorrow and see just what
        else is inside.
            (winks as he folds steps)
        However, tonight's for free.
        I plan on some fun. Brown

hair and hazel eyes type of
fun.

INT. STATEROOM - NIGHT

Two people are occupied in a very nice
stateroom. The bed is in the center of
the floor. While the grunts travel in
storage, this is a first-class cabin. The
lights are subtle but not out. The sheets
are shiny and caramel colored. There is a
man, the CARGO HANDLER, and a WOMAN
underneath in the final throes of passion.
The woman is very active and on top of the
man.

As the woman finishes and snuggles under
the man's chin, sleepiness pulls her
eyelids down.

                WOMAN IN BED
             (softly)
          We've had each other for a
          wonderful night, and I don't
          even know your name. Care
          to share it with me?

We see him lean his face into her hair,
drawing himself to her, beginning the
rocking of a tender embrace.

                CARGO HANDLER
          Does it really matter? This
          moment is all that counts.

And, sure enough, after a few minutes, we
see that what he said becomes true as the
sheets begin to move once again.

MONTAGE:

INT.   READY TO DISEMBARK - DAY

Multiple scenes show:

A flotilla readying itself to land on a planet with unknown decimation.

Transports are readied.

Cargo crates are relabeled with new manifest lists.

Luxury goods are stowed and working clothes donned.

Groggy grunts have packs slapped on their chests.

People with three weeks of intimacy are now suddenly pulled back into themselves, distant from those they were intimate with over the course of the trip.

ACT XIX - LANDING PARTY

EXT. LANDING CRAFT - DAY

A landing craft sets down in a verdant
area. The ship is in a clearing with
taller growth all around. There are very
few tree-like structures, and they are
very low. Outside the craft, we see
military readiness is high. Men with
weapons on point station themselves around
the landing craft. BRAXTN is holding up a
scanner looking for heat signatures.

>   BRAXTN
> First approach team on the
> ground, Braxtn speaking.
> All seems clear. Will check
> back in five. Out.

>   SHIP (Off Screen)
> Acknowledged. Will wait for
> check. Out.

>   BRAXTN
>   (to his men)
> Clear! Secondary postures.
>   (to himself)
> God, this is beautiful! The

colors, so saturated,
intense. I've never seen
green fields this brilliant
before!
     (looking up at the twin suns low on
     opposing horizons)
Who would have expected
that, a stunning yellow sky?
My god, this must be the
old-Earth Eden my old great-
grandmother used to tell me
stories about. This is a
breath of fresh air to me.
I can almost feel my youth
again. What was MegaCorp
fighting for here on this
beautiful planet that caused
them to wipe out the entire
population?
     (pause)
If only someone could be
found here who lived through
the genocide.
     (pause, then with a change in
     expression)
What a treat the other teams
have in store for them.
     (to ship)
First approach team clear.
Moving forward. In five.
Out.

          SHIP (Off Screen)
Acknowledged. Waiting.
Out.

MONTAGE:

The great landers begin settling
themselves around the planet.

Giant construction landers bring mighty pieces of equipment to put previously known infrastructure back into prime condition.

Transport landers ferry workers to their various locales across the planet.

Survey teams begin cataloguing the resources of the planet.

EXT. VERDANT TRAIL BESIDE THE SEA - DAY

NALT'N, maybe nineteen, is a PACK GRUNT with a SURVEY TEAM. His job is to carry the packs. He is not quite keeping up. He rests his hand on a boulder, glancing down just in time to see a damp, bare footprint fade from the surface of a flat stone. He freezes. In a very tight, almost inaudible voice, he calls out.

> NALT'N, PACK GRUNT
> Hey, guys.
> (louder)
> Guys, you need to see this.
> (vision goes black and collapses)

> MULTIPLE VOICES
> Where did Nalt'n go? He was just here. There he is. Is he okay?

LATER THAT DAY:

> NALT'N, PACK GRUNT
> (earnestly)
> No, it was right there.
> (points to the stone)

A footprint. Wet. It just faded away as I watched.

                    TEAMMATE
          Like this?

The teammate wets his boot, placing it on the dry stone, leaving the imprint of its treads, the marks fading as they dry.

Nalt'n realizes what has startled him so. He grabs his own boot, pulls it off, strips his sock off, and stumbles to the water. He slaps his bare foot into the water and hops back to the team. The team watches him place his wet foot solidly on the selected stone. He lifts his foot, and the teams sees the water begin to fade.

                    NALT'N, PACK GRUNT
                      (emphatically)
          No! Like that!

Hands pull out comm units and portable 'glasses,' the messages sent being the same. The smiles on their faces say that hope has returned to the teams on Se'Yan't.

EXT. BASE CAMP - DAY

BRAXTN spins his glass around in his hand. He stops spinning it, showing an image from a report on top, a watery footprint on stone. He turns to the TEAM LEADER at his side.

                    TEAM LEADER
          I don't know, ser. The

reports just keep coming in.
Who would have put any real
credence into that footprint
sighting? The guy was just
a grunt. No credentials.
No verification by anyone
else on his team. Just his
word. And he was passed out
when the team found him.
Bizarre. Now.

She shakes her head, takes the 'glass,'
and flips the 'glass' through the reports,
hundreds of them. Catching one, she pulls
it back to the front.

          TEAM LEADER (CONT'D)
Like this one, ser. The
prints seem to come right
out of the water. See?

She flicks the image, one edge of it
jumping out at them.

          TEAM LEADER (CONT'D)
You can see it right here.
There's the water, then
there's the first print.
And another thing, ser.
None of these prints, not
any of them found at *any* of
the sites are adult size.
My best guess as to the age?
Eight to maybe ten local
years. And that's been
verified by our sociological
survey division. There's a
Ser Alb't deFralin. He's a
full SSM.rl, so you can't
fault his credentials. He

assures me these prints
cannot come from one of our
teams. He pulled up the
stats on this entire
mission, and not even the
smallest of our females has
feet this size. I just
don't know, ser. Like I
said earlier, bizarre.

She turns to her 'glass,' the reports
sliding under her fingers as she shakes
her head; to herself she repeats her
words.

                    TEAM LEADER (CONT'D)
          I just don't know.

EXT. VERDANT TRAIL BESIDE THE SEA - DAY

ALB'T DEFRALIN walks into the middle of
things and points.

                    DEFRALIN
          Just behind that large rock.
          Yes, right there. Good.
          Aim it to pan this entire
          beach area. If anything
          passes here, we'll get to
          see it on the glass. Good
          work, team.

DeFralin turns, an AIDE tugging at his
sleeve finally getting his attention.

                    DEFRALIN (CONT'D)
          Great solar suns, what is
          wrong with you, dancing
          there like your feet are on
          fire?

                    AIDE
        You won't believe this, ser.
        You might as well take all
        this back with you. You
        don't need it anymore. All
        these sightings? Well,
        there's more. So much more.
        The latest reports flooding
        in aren't on the coasts
        anymore. They're coming in
        from *everywhere*. Just check
        the glass, ser.

A 'glass' is handed to deFralin. A
message is on the glass.

A very readable, though somewhat
transparent image of a note on a 'glass'
being handed to someone is transposed over
deFralin and his aide. Braxtn reads the
note aloud in a voice over.

*From Security Chief A'man Braxtn. To
Sociological Team Leader Ser Alb't
deFralin, SSM.rl. Please view the
following attachments offering insights as
to the possible meanings of the alleged
sightings being reported across Se'Yan't.
I have culled this information from many
hours of research pulled from sources
spanning centuries. I firmly believe that
all rumors are based on kernels of fact.
Although the fountain of youth was only a
myth on old-Earth, this is not old-Earth.
Please look for the facts inside and they
may help you make progress toward the
answers you seek.*

The note fades from view to show deFralin

looking at the glass.

                    DEFRALIN
          What if it could be true?

                    AIDE
          What, ser. Is everything
          all right?

                    DEFRALIN
               (startled by the aide's question)
          Nothing. Just the wishful
          fantasy of an old scholar
          who's already chased too
          many empty dreams in his
          career. I will be fine.
          Just keep up the good job
          you're doing for us, son.

DeFralin turns back to the glass, his
sureness of reality tempering his desires.
He closes his eyes for a moment, and
whispers to himself.

                    DEFRALIN (CONT'D)
          What if it really could be
          true?

DeFralin takes a deep, deep breath, and
slips the glass into his tunic.

                    DEFRALIN (CONT'D)
          Okay, team. Let's pull it
          all down. The real
          excitement has moved on.
          Let's head inland.

At the water's surface, the forehead and
eyes of several children break the surface
and go back under.

INT. ROOM IN THE CITY - DAY

A worker is talking with deFralin. He is
gesturing around a partially refurbished
room.

> WORKER
> Now, ser, I was in this
> building yesterday. This
> simply wasn't here. You
> know it never gets really
> dark here, at least not in
> the months we've been
> involved in this survey,
> what with the nearest
> eclipse not being until
> several months away. But we
> do plan a night in our
> schedules. You know, there
> are only so many people on
> each team. Well, we are in
> the process of refurbishing
> this series of buildings.
> With the city vacated for
> eight years, things have
> been let go, you know. This
> is the building my team was
> working in just yesterday.
> I tell you, none of this was
> here.

DeFralin's excitement is clear on his
face. He sees discarded plant materials.
Food stuffs. Things children would leave
behind.

INT. BASE CAMP - DAY

An irritated look settles on
deFralin's face as he tries to work

at his desk. A commotion outside
causes him to look up repeatedly.
DeFralin stands to stomp outside and
silence the noise.

He stops as his 'glass' on the desk
chimes. He reaches his hand to touch the
'glass,' and Braxtn's face appears,
glancing back and forth, his attention on
two things at once.

> BRAXTN
> (breathless, he barks his words)
> Get out here, deFralin.
> This is your moment to
> shine. They're *here*.

> DEFRALIN
> (opening the door)
> Great gods!

DeFralin steps outside to hundreds of
beautiful, golden-skinned godlets of the
same apparent age, both boys and girls,
and each one is totally naked.

FLASHBACK:

EXT. ROCKY BEACH — DAY (EIGHT YEARS
EARLIER)

Rjorck lies on the beach, his body broken,
breath barely in his body. There are
glimpses of obvious damage from MegaCorp's
atrocities visible in the background. The
waters of the sea are lapping at his body.

MONTAGE:

The water is rising on Rjorck.

Rjorck is under water, his eyes closed.

Suddenly his eyes open.

Nearly transparent, a number of favorite
scenes of Rjorck's memories overlay his
image, the eyes always seen.

Rjorck's body disappears from view, the
clarity of the water remaining, with only
a slight distortion showing where he must
still be.

EIGHT YEARS LATER IN THE SAME LOCATION:

The stones line the beach. The damage
from MegaCorp's atrocities has been
cleared away. The waters are blue. The
sky is yellow. The vegetation is green.
One sun hangs high in the sky. The other
brushes the horizon. A disturbance rises
in the water. When the water peels away,
a golden-skinned boy of about eight rises
to walk on the beach. He looks around and
arches his neck. He continues to stand as
others begin to rise from the sea to join
him.

The boy's eyes look around as if at a long
unseen but not forgotten memory. His
mouth forms the shape of his planet's
name, testing its feel. Then his mouth
starts to move one more time.

            BOY
    Se'Yan't.

Children now line the beach as far as the
eye can see, all eight years old.

EXT.   BASE CAMP - DAY

DEFRALIN reaches and takes a 'glass' being
handed to him. He looks at it for a few
moments, manipulating the contents. He
then looks up.

                DEFRALIN
Are there more?
    (flips through the glass)
Look at this one. It's
exactly the same as the one
I was sent from the southern
continent. Here.

DeFralin calls out to his sociological
team and holds out the glass with two
examples displayed.

                DEFRALIN (CONT'D)
Check this out. The one on
the left was sent in two
weeks ago. It came from the
south. Now look at this one
that just came in from a
local group. There is no
difference. These are
children.

He looks at his team, their expressions as
mystified as his.

                DEFRALIN (CONT'D)
Racial memory? This is your
field, people. Give me some
answers.
    (waves them away)

OLLEN walks up to deFralin with an

expectant grin on his face.

                    OLLEN
          Ssm. deFralin?
            (sees deFralin turn to him)
          I'm sure you have been
          apprised of the situation
          here.

                    DEFRALIN
          I'm sorry. I don't
          understand what you mean.

                    OLLEN
          Ser, these children are
          obviously indigenous. Do
          you understand what that
          means? This world is
          theirs.

                    DEFRALIN
          And that means . . .

                    OLLEN
          We must document them.
          Children! Have you totaled
          the reported number seen so
          far? It's in the thousands.

                    DEFRALIN
          I plan to do just that.
          What is your point, and who
          are you?

                    OLLEN
            (smiles wider)
          We are all here on
          MegaCorp's meal ticket. You
          see, everyone thought this
          planet's population was

decimated. Yet, here we
have thousands of live
Rejuvies roaming the planet.
With proper documentation,
surely it can be proven that
MegaCorp was not the
aggressor in this situation.
Damages can then be limited
to basic restoration of the
planetary infrastructure,
and the punitive damages can
be dismissed. If you can
help me, I'm sure MegaCorp
will find a way to reward
you in the future.

    DEFRALIN
  (instantly lashes out)
Away from me! How dare you
try to coerce me into
twisting this situation to
MegaCorp's benefit!

He steps toward the man, pulling his
'glass' from his pocket.

    DEFRALIN (CONT'D)
I am contacting the security
chief at this very moment.
How dare you claim to be
here as part of this effort
to restore the damages
inflicted on this
civilization!

LATER:

Braxtn and deFralin stand together with
angry looks on their faces.

                    BRAXTN
              (glares at Ollen's back as he is
              taken away)
          My most sincere apologies,
          Ssm. deFralin. I have had
          my eye on both this man and
          a partner of his for the
          entire mission. This is the
          first opportunity they've
          given me to haul their butts
          off for deportation back to
          the main transport. They'll
          be in slow-sleep cubicles
          quicker than they can blink,
          I'll tell you that.
              (pauses, watching the man being
              confined on the ground transport)
          Feel free to contact me at
          any time.
              (shakes his hand)

As he heads after the rest of the security
team, Braxtn continues to chew himself out
under his breath.

                    BRAXTN
          Devil curse that Ollen and
          his partner, Ens't. I knew
          something like this would
          happen when I saw their
          names on the list . . .

INT. BASE CAMP - DAY

A COLLEAGUE is flipping through poems on
deFralin's glass.

                    COLLEAGUE
          These are really good,
          Alb't. How many of these do

you have?

                    DEFRALIN
At last count, more than
eight hundred, and there are
more still coming in. Not
as rapidly as at first, but
I still see several new ones
a week.

                    COLLEAGUE
They're all documented?
Every one?

                    DEFRALIN
I only officially track
those coming in from
multiple locations. Every
example is documented with
the location, the time, and
the person who recorded it.
Look at this one here. It
came in from seventeen
locations, nearly all
simultaneously. Listen:

*When the fire above falls
from space,
Water below is the safest
place.
Land in-between is where
death is sure,
Se'Yan't's oceans will make
us pure.
Let us live in peace again.*

                    COLLEAGUE
Cryptic, wouldn't you say?
What do you make of it?

DEFRALIN
I've puzzled over that but
can't seem to make a
connection.

COLLEAGUE
Are they all like this?

DEFRALIN
Cryptic? Pretty much.
    (scrolls through several more)
See? Look at this one.
    (hands the glass over for the other
    to see)
Read it.

COLLEAGUE
Old age, old age,
You wait for me.
When life is through,
I'll see the sea.
Return, return,
Life lives again,
My youth renewed,
I'll walk on land.
    (pausing)
There must be some meaning
behind them.

DEFRALIN
    (retrieves his glass, pauses)
Almost like a chant.
Fascinating, though. I've
inquired as to the
possibility of publishing
the collection with any
proceeds going directly back
to the children. Once
MegaCorp steps back from
this salvage mission, these

guys are going to need some
help. That's the other
thing I can't seem to get
past. Why no adults?

>   COLLEAGUE
> Why not, Alb't? Is it
> possible the populace knew
> what was coming and hid
> their children away for
> safety?

>   DEFRALIN
> Possible, perhaps. Yeah,
> it's certainly possible, but
> *thousands*? It's just hard
> to explain away.

DeFralin runs his finger across the
surface of his glass, the information
inside flickering as it tries to guess
what he wants, mumbles as his colleague
steps away.

>   DEFRALIN (CONT'D)
> I couldn't prove it,
> wouldn't even try. It would
> be career death for sure.
> But I can come up with only
> one scenario that comes even
> close to offering a
> plausible explanation, and
> Braxtn has given me that.
>   (without humor)
> Thanks, Braxtn!

DeFralin stares at the shifting images on
the glass in his hand, none of them clear,
all of them simply possibilities.

DEFRALIN (CONT'D)
Thanks for nothing, Braxtn.

THE END

Read all the books in this vibrant new series!

The Se'Yan't Chronicles

Get Yours At:
www.ThreeSkilletPublishing.com

THREE SKILLET

www.ingramcontent.com/pod-product-compliance
Lightning Source LLC
Chambersburg PA
CBHW070838250626
47159CB00003B/834